Donated by
Floyd Dickman

Your Eyes in Stars

BOOKS BY M. E. KERR

SNAKES DON'T MISS THEIR MOTHERS

SLAP YOUR SIDES
2002 Books for the Teen Age (New York Public Library)
2002 ALA *Booklist* Editors' Choice

WHAT BECAME OF HER
2001 Books for the Teen Age (New York Public Library)

BLOOD ON THE FOREHEAD: WHAT I KNOW ABOUT WRITING
1998 Books for the Teen Age (New York Public Library)

DELIVER US FROM EVIE
1995 Best Books for Young Adults (ALA)
1995 Recommended Books for
Reluctant Young Adult Readers (ALA)
1995 Fanfare Honor List (*The Horn Book*)
1995 Books for the Teen Age (New York Public Library)
1994 *School Library Journal* Best Books of the Year
1994 ALA *Booklist* Books for Youth Editors' Choices
1994 Best Books Honor (Michigan Library Association)

LINGER
1994 Books for the Teen Age (New York Public Library)

FELL DOWN
1991 ALA *Booklist* Books for Youth Editors' Choices
1992 Books for the Teen Age (New York Public Library)

FELL BACK
1990 Edgar Allan Poe Award Finalist (Mystery Writers of America)
1990 Books for the Teen Age (New York Public Library)

FELL

1987 Best Books for Young Adults (ALA)

1987 ALA *Booklist* Books for Youth Editors' Choice

1988 Books for the Teen Age (New York Public Library)

NIGHT KITES

1991 California Young Reader Medal

Best of the Best Books (YA) 1966–1986 (ALA)

1987 Recommended Books for
Reluctant Young Adult Readers (ALA)

ALA *Booklist*'s "Best of the '80s"

LITTLE LITTLE

1981 Notable Children's Books (ALA)

1981 Best Books for Young Adults (ALA)

1981 *School Library Journal* Best Books of the Year

1981 Golden Kite Award (Society of Children's Book Writers)

1982 Books for the Teen Age (New York Public Library)

GENTLEHANDS

Best of the Best Books (YA) 1966–1992 (ALA)

1978 *School Library Journal* Best Books of the Year

1978 Christopher Award

1978 Outstanding Children's Books of the Year
(*The New York Times*)

1979 Books for the Teen Age (New York Public Library)

IF I LOVE YOU, AM I TRAPPED FOREVER?

1973 Outstanding Children's Books of the Year
(*The New York Times*)

1973 Child Study Association's Children's Book of the Year

1973 *Book World*'s Children's Spring Book Festival Honor Book

DINKY HOCKER SHOOTS SMACK!

Best of the Best Books (YA) 1970–1983 (ALA)

1972 Notable Children's Books (ALA)

1972 *School Library Journal* Best Books of the Year

Best Children's Books of 1972 (Library of Congress)

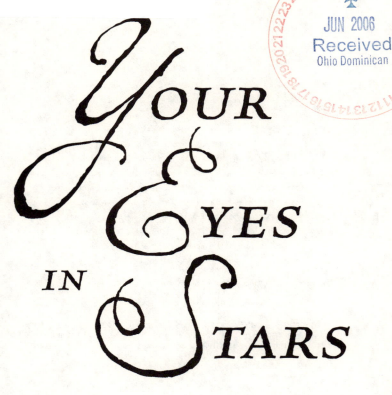

Your Eyes in Stars

A NOVEL BY

M. E. KERR

HarperCollins*Publishers*

Translation of "As Much as You Can" from the original
Greek graciously provided by Marina Padakis

Library of Congress Cataloging-in-Publication Data
Kerr, M. E.
    Your eyes in stars : a novel / by M. E. Kerr.— 1st ed.
      p. cm.
    Summary: In their small New York town, two teenaged girls
become friends while helping each other make sense of their families, their neighbors, and themselves as they approach adulthood in
the years preceding World War II.
    ISBN-10: 0-06-075682-9 (trade bdg.) — ISBN-13: 978-0-06-075682-6
(trade bdg.)
    ISBN-10: 0-06-075683-7 (lib. bdg.) — ISBN-13: 978-0-06-075683-3
(lib. bdg.)
    [1. Friendship—Fiction. 2. Conduct of life—Fiction. 3. City and
town life—New York (State)—New York—Fiction. 4. Family life—
New York (State)—Fiction. 5. New York (State)—History—20th
century—Fiction. 6. United States—History—1933–1945—Fiction.
7. World War, 1939–1945—Fiction.] I. Title.
PZ7.K46825You 2006
[Fic]—dc22   2005008781
                                                                   CIP
                                                                    AC

Typography by Karin Paprocki
1 2 3 4 5 6 7 8 9 10
❖
First Edition

FOR PETER D. SIERUTA,

FRIEND AND FELLOW WRITER

YOUR EYES IN STARS

PART ONE

1

JESSIE MYRER

I DIDN'T BELIEVE anyone was actually afraid of the prison.
When kids were little, along with spankings, they'd get
warnings they were going to end up there if they didn't
behave. But nobody in town really feared the place. That's
what I thought.

You saw the prison before you saw the town. It looked
like a fort sprawled across eighteen acres on Retribution
Hill. It was a small city itself, surrounded by a wall thirty
feet high and ringed by guards in sentry boxes at the top.
They were ready with high-powered rifles. But after my
father became warden, townspeople commented that it
seemed more like a prep school than a penitentiary. The
black-and-white striped uniforms were changed to light-
blue ones. The prison band named The Blues became
famous in Cayuta County, often appearing in public at

Joyland Park in Cayuta or during local parades down Main Street. More and more people didn't say *the prison*; it began to be called The Hill.

All the other kids who had fathers or mothers working at the prison went four years to Cayuta High West and took courses like Shop and Motor Repair, Typing and Shorthand. At Cayuta High East, where my brother and I were sent, we learned Latin and geometry, French and English composition. After High West you got a job; after High East you went to college.

Three years before, when we first arrived in Cayuta from Elmira Reformatory, my mother reigned over the wives of guards and groundskeepers like a queen. It took her a while to realize this town was different. Prison people weren't high-class. In this town she wasn't royalty of any kind in the eyes of the community. She was nothing, though she herself had said sometimes she felt like "next to nothing," never missing an opportunity to take a step up.

My dad was not a golfer, and he wasn't a sailor, so we Myers weren't members of the country club or the yacht club. Oh, that wasn't the only reason we weren't. Both my brother and I realized that, and so did my mother. If my father was aware of it, it didn't faze him.

At High East, my brother, Seth, had no problem getting

along since he had a build for both basketball and football. He also had a fan, one of those kids who trailed after him and was the only other person in town besides my mother who cut out of the newspapers all the write-ups about him on the sports page of *The Cayuta Advertizer*. His name was Richard Nolan, and he was my buddy too. We hung out at lunch, eating our sandwiches in the parking lot or on cold days on the stairs near the gym.

Sometimes when Richard was sick or had to go to the orthodontist in nearby Syracuse, New York, I'd walk down Retribution Hill and eat lunch at home.

I'd tell him, "Mother thinks I won't eat in the cafeteria because the Chi Pis snub me." I called those sorority girls the Cowpies.

"Tell her you're just not gregarious. That's a good word, gregarious."

Richard could always tell you what you were or weren't; he prided himself on being a wordsmith.

Rumor had it that J. J. Joy, president of Chi Theta Pi, had called me "tacky" and fought for a 100-percent blackball of me. She'd said I should have gone to High West with others like me.

Richard blamed her blackball of me on her father's rule that she could not date until she was seventeen.

"It's made her bitter and mean," he said.

Over and over Richard and I would moan to each other:

"What's to become of us?" Richard wanted to be a writer, which his father said was "a limpwrist ambition." Seth said *limpwrist* meant "effeminate," and Richard should ask his father how effeminate he thought Rudyard Kipling was or Jack London. . . . Still, I didn't have a clue what would become of me. Maybe I would end up living with my parents like Marlene Hellman, and everyone talked about it. Everyone called her Mayonnaise and said she would always be a child, even though she worked at the telephone company and was a champion bridge player.

I had just finished writing in my diary: "Suicide would be the answer if it wasn't so hard and painful to do." I didn't really mean it. I hadn't even figured out a way to do it. But it gave me a certain satisfaction to record the thought. Diaries aren't meant for good tidings.

That was the day and the very moment when everything about my boring life would change. This was when my mother called up to me, "Jess? Our neighbor Elisa Stadler is on her way up to your room."

The emphasis was on the last name, Stadler. It was a new name to my mother, and already the sound of it was filled with awe and portent.

2

I'LL NEVER FORGET meeting her that first afternoon, the little sideways grin on her face, the sparkle in her eyes as though we were friends who got a kick out of each other, even though we hadn't yet spoken.

The Stadlers were the only family from Germany in our small town. There were the Schwitters, of course, but they had lived so long on Lakeview Avenue they were considered Cayutians. Unlike any other in Cayuta, their house was enormous, hidden behind a wall, overlooking Cayuta Lake. Reinhardt Schwitter was the sole person that famous or rich who had ever lived in Cayuta. Maybe in the whole state of New York.

Despite the fact the Stadlers had been across the street since the week before Christmas, I hadn't introduced myself.

"March yourself over there and welcome her to the neighborhood," my mother would plead.

7

I was too shy. I was glad when shortly after that my mother did an about-face, mumbling something about certain people preferring to keep to themselves.

Sometimes I would hear Elisa Stadler's phonograph at night, as though it were set down next to the window in her room, both the volume and the window up, but I had no proof of that. Elisa was fifteen, a year older than I was, and believed to be a snob by everyone at High East.

"I heard you have a push on John Dillinger," Elisa said without so much as a hello, but the grin was a big smile now, a real white one. Good teeth. Dimples.

"What's a push?"

"Don't you have a smash on one of your gangsters?"

I bent double laughing. She would always affect me that way, make me see the fun of things, even when the joke was on her.

"A crush. You mean a crush," I said. "John Dillinger isn't one of my gangsters. He's the main one. He was the most wanted until they caught him. If you came from this country, you'd realize how big he is!"

We stood in my bedroom under one of the wanted posters I had tacked to my wall. My brother, Seth, was struggling with some inner darkness that made him shun all that he had once cherished. He had given his gangster posters to me, even the ones of Bonnie and Clyde, which he had once hung above his desk in his room.

GET DILLINGER!
$15,000 REWARD
GET HIM
DEAD
OR ALIVE

There were two photographs of John Dillinger, one facing front and one side view.

"He can put his shoes under my bed any day," I said. It was something Seth used to say about the Hollywood star Ginger Rogers. She can put her shoes under my bed any day.

"Why would he put his shoes under your bed?" Elisa said.

"It's just an expression. He's sharp, so he's sexy, so he can put his shoes under my bed any day."

She shrugged. "Your Dillinger is very handsome but not to my taste." Although she told me later that she had learned English almost as soon as she could walk, her *v*'s were always pronounced like *w*'s, and her *w*'s came out like *v*'s. *He is wary handsome*. Other things made me smile too. My last name came out of her mouth as *Mywah*.

"Why isn't Dillinger to your taste?" I asked.

"I don't fancy criminals," said Elisa.

It was well known at High East that the Myrer kids collected the wanted posters of famous outlaws. It was our little claim to fame. Both Seth and I had presented them at show-and-tells. I always kept one inside my locker, on the door. Dillinger was the current one. Of all of the gangsters, John Dillinger, famous bank robber, was my favorite and the easiest one to trade for a movie poster.

"Our whole country roots for Dillinger," I said. "Everyone's poor because the banks are taking away their homes, their savings, everything. My father says John Dillinger gets revenge for them."

My father had said something like that, but not that. He would never make a criminal seem like a hero.

"I didn't cross the street to talk about John Dillinger," said Elisa Stadler. "I came to give you an invitation. You know Reinhardt Schwitter, don't you?"

"I know who he is. Who doesn't?"

"Mr. Schwitter is donating a film Holy Family Church will show to the community, in their auditorium. I'm going."

"And?" I couldn't believe I was being invited somewhere with Elisa Stadler after weeks of being right across the street without a hello. I had my hands on my hips, eyeing her suspiciously, but we were both somehow amused by each other. We could see that in each other's eyes.

"And I was wondering if you would go to see the film with me," said Elisa.

I was in blue jeans with one of Seth's old shirts worn outside. Elisa wore a plaid pleated skirt and red cardigan.

We were both blondes, but I was what was known as a dishwater blonde, and Elisa's hair was the kind you saw in Halo shampoo ads. It fell to her shoulders, soft-looking, straight.

"What film is it?"

"It's called *All Quiet on the Western Front*," said Elisa.

"Never heard of it."

"My father says it's excellent."

"Who's in it?"

"He's a new Hollywood star named Lew Ayres. I've seen a picture of him. If you think your John Dillinger is something, wait until you see Lew Ayres. Will you go with me Saturday night the twenty-seventh?"

"I don't have any other plans," I admitted. My "plans" were mostly things I decided to do a half hour beforehand.

I picked up a copy of *True Confessions*, to use as a fan and also to keep Elisa from seeing it. It was a magazine belonging to my mother. It promised weary housewives risqué stories of women running off with other women's husbands, lost virginity, and babies born out of wedlock. I had tucked it out of sight. I didn't want Elisa Stadler thinking I read stories like "A Night of Rapture Ruined Me."

Even though it was almost below zero outside, I felt warm and glad I'd had the magazine for a fan. Glad she was there, too, even though she made me slightly self-conscious. At High East, Elisa Stadler stood for glamour and sophistication. She wasn't this great beauty. It was her accent, all the languages she could speak, and the foreign places she had lived. Elisa's blue eyes met my own with confidence and curiosity.

I was still in my tomboy stage. I couldn't look anyone in the eye for very long, unless it was Richard Nolan. I wore Seth's vests and caps, and part of my act was to pretend that the last thing I would ever do in my entire life was join the Cowpie sorority girls after school at Hollywood Hangout. There they'd be, all of them, wearing their diamond-shaped pins, crowded into booths, ordering peanut sundaes and Cokes, playing the nickelodeon, swooning over the songs and the boys hanging out by the counter. I longed to be back in Elmira, where everyone knew my name, my dad was respected, and I'd planned to live my entire life.

"Where is your brother?" Elisa asked.

"He's not home." I should have said, "You'll find him somewhere in front of a mirror." This was around the same time it had first registered with Seth that he didn't look like other boys. He looked a lot better. It seemed to me that it had happened overnight. He had stepped into his own little world. He had even given me his scrapbooks filled with newspaper clippings of gangsters holding up banks, or gunning each other down, and sometimes being gunned down themselves.

In his early teens Seth had such hideous hickeys, he would cover his face with calamine lotion at night. Then, miraculously, the change when he was seventeen. "Seth?" I would say, feigning astonishment when schoolmates said he was "sharp." But I knew what they meant.

"I better go home now," Elisa said.

"Okay."

"I'll see you Saturday the twenty-seventh."

"Okay."

And that was how it all began.

3

MOVIES IN THE cellar at Holy Family were frantic affairs with the priests running up and down the aisles, making sure teenagers weren't sitting too close or God forbid necking.

Richard Nolan was there with his father, a levy bailiff who was not very popular in Cayuta. He had the job of repossessing automobiles whose owners couldn't afford the monthly payments. There were more and more cars being hauled away. It was just another example of how the Depression was affecting everyone, even the Joys. They were one of the most prominent families in our town.

That night, when Richard came over to say hello, he asked us if we knew what these seven words had in common: *act, ample, it, plain, port, position,* and *press.*

"I will never guess it," said Elisa.

"Give up, Jessie?"

"I give up," I said.

"They all form new words when the prefix *ex* is added," Richard said. *"Exact, example, explain—"* He held his hands up. "See?"

"Who cares about that?" I said.

Elisa said, "Me. I love games with words."

"Then you're going to love Richard!" I said.

Richard fled.

Before the movie began, Father Lardo made a little speech, a bawling out, really, intended for someone in the audience.

"I don't know to whom I'm speaking," he said, "but I have an idea you know who you are, and I have an idea you're here tonight."

Father Lardo liked to wear mufti whenever he could, instead of the white collar. He wore a black sweater and black jeans, with a bright-red muffler wrapped around his neck.

"Someone pushed Mr. Nolan's Buick down Retribution Hill last night before he could impound a new Oldsmobile belonging to Horace Joy. Whoever you are, don't think you can get away with this. You broke the law! Okay, no one likes these automobile impoundments. They're humiliating to the owners. It seems like an unfair law. But remember"—Father Lardo shook his finger at the audience—"an outlaw is far, far worse than a bad law."

"Who would do such a thing?" Elisa asked me.

I knew who would, but I would never give Richard away. Because his father was the levy bailiff, he always knew what car was being confiscated, what night. Three or four times he'd secretly foiled his father's plans to take another car.

I said, "Last night they were going after Mr. Joy's car. He doesn't have an enemy in the world, so any number of us could have done it." I shouldn't have included myself. My enemy in the Cowpies was Mr. Joy's daughter, J. J. I liked him just fine, but I'd never do anything to make life easier for her family.

"Who is this Mr. Joy?" Elisa said.

"A big shot," I said. "He owned Joystep Shoes before he got wiped out in the stock market crash. A lot of Cayutians are out of jobs now."

Just as the film was about to start, Wolfgang Schwitter made his grand entrance.

"That's Reinhardt Schwitter's son," I said. "Wolfgang. He's the tall one. He's the oldest."

"How old? He seems very old. In his twenties?"

"Eighteen, nineteen. He's just very sure of himself."

Wolfgang was turning in every direction, bowing, waving, smiling, just as though he were the star of the evening, not this Lew Ayres of Hollywood, California.

"He is handsome," said Elisa.

"We say sharp," I said. "He's very sharp."

"Yes," she said, hugging herself because they never heated the cellar before the audience got there, and maybe Elisa felt a chill go through her too, at the sight of him.

Wolfgang was at his best that winter night. He had on a belted camel's hair coat, these tight brown flannel pants that grabbed his ankles, showing just a peek of his argyle socks and shiny penny loafers. There was snow on the sidewalks outside, but typically Wolfgang strode through it without boots, no cap over his thick, curly black hair, a light-brown scarf to match his eyes. I'd seen him in his new blue Nash Rambler with the rumble seat, top down in any kind of weather, radio playing loud. Look at me. Look at me. . . . Who wouldn't? I always thought.

Wolfgang's brother, Dieter, was with him. Dieter was younger, my age. He was the opposite of his brother. Mousy, drab, short. It was well known around town that Wolfgang wanted to become a New York Broadway actor. Of all things, Dieter wanted to be an accompanist. He would settle for sitting on a piano bench while a whole theater of fans applauded a singer, a violinist, or some other performer with his name featured at the top of the program.

"Is your brother here?" Elisa asked just before the lights dimmed.

"These days he's doing a disappearing act," I said. At least I never saw him. I was amazed when Richard told me that Seth had been in on last night's rescue of Mr. Joy's Oldsmobile. *Rescue* was Richard's word for it, of course. My mother said that Richard was a "bleeding heart." She didn't mean it in a nice way, but I thought there was something fine about Richard's way of helping people, some he didn't know at all. Richard had given one of his good winter jackets to a tramp last November, when the snow came down day after day, relentlessly.

"QUIET!" Father Lardo barked.

The movie had begun.

4

I<small>T WAS A</small> grim movie about the World War, the fate of several young men who fought in it, and one who opposed it. I didn't like war movies, but Elisa said since this new leader, Hitler, was gaining popularity in Germany, she should learn about it. Hitler could cause a war, she said.

Afterward we were hurried out of the cellar, almost as if Father Lardo wanted to wash his hands of acting as a chaperon for a few dozen teenagers. Outside, a bus from Paris Arts & Science waited to return preppies and their profs.

Once again Wolfgang Schwitter stationed himself in a prominent place, as though he were the host of the occasion. He stood on the top step of Holy Family Church as we all climbed the stairs and filed out the front door.

"Hello? Wolfgang? Wolfgang Schwitter?" Elisa said to him.

"What is it?" He had to bend over to talk to her, he was so tall.

"I'm Heinz Stadler's daughter. I'm Elisa."

"How do you do," he said, bowing but not offering his hand; all the while he was looking around at everyone but her.

"I guess you don't know my name," Elisa said.

"Well, now I do," he said, and for a brief moment he gave her the benefit of his smile, which any toothpaste company would be proud to feature in its ads.

It was one of those moments when you wanted to smash someone's face in for being so rude and careless about someone you were rooting for. There were times since we'd first moved to Cayuta I'd even feel sorry for myself. I'd be sitting in the cafeteria at a table with other girls, all talking, no one meeting my eyes. My eyes would be searching theirs, beseeching theirs: Notice me. That was before I'd learned to turn the tables: Never look at them, be the loner, the snob, whatever it took. . . . I wished Elisa had never spoken to him.

Then Wolfgang noticed the gold dachshund pin Elisa had fixed to the collar of her coat. "Excuse me," he said. "Could you possibly think of selling me your pin? I know it's a strange request, but we just lost our dachshund, and that would be some solace to my mother."

"I can't. It's my grandmother's pin."

"Oh well . . . I tried."

"Yes, you did."

"Then good night, Phyllis."

He turned away, and Elisa and I walked along Genesee Street together, a light snow falling, so cold out we could see our breaths in front of us. Elisa with furry earmuffs and I with red, burning ears.

I wanted to blot out what had just happened, not mention it the same as I wouldn't want someone to see and hear me being humiliated.

"If you want to know what I think of him," I said, "I think he's a seven on a scale of one to ten."

"Lower," Elisa said.

"Lower? You were the one raving about him."

"Oh. Lew Ayres," she said. "Why only a seven?"

"Who did you think I meant?"

"I thought you meant Wolfgang Schwitter," she said. "He called me Phyllis, did you hear that? He doesn't spend much time making conversation, does he?"

"He's that way with everyone. I don't think he even knows my name." I didn't think he was that way with everyone, but I knew he didn't know my name.

Elisa said, "More even than how someone looks, I count how someone acts toward you. That Richard Nolan we met tonight? He knows how to make you feel welcome."

I didn't tell her she shouldn't take that personally, either. Richard really was that way with everyone unless the person was mean to animals or unkind to misfits, paupers, and losers.

"How come you got those movie tickets from Mr. Schwitter?" I asked Elisa.

"My father knows him. Reinhardt Schwitter is a pacifist, like my father."

"The way Lew Ayres was in the movie?"

"Yes. And the way I am too. And my father."

"If we ever had a war, I might be one too," I said.

"*Bitte! Bitte!*" she said, which I would hear often from her, a German way of expressing exasperation with something or someone, the way we'd say, "Oh, please!" She stopped herself from laughing. "You are not a pacifist! With all those gangster posters? They kill people, those gangsters."

"I don't collect the gangsters. I collect the posters."

"I'm surprised your family lets you hang up posters like that."

"My father gets them for me," I said.

But I decided that in the beginning the less she knew about my family, the better. I already sensed there were vast differences between us, starting there.

I said, "I heard your father's a farmer." My mother had heard that. He was thin and dapper, with wavy brown hair and blue eyes the color of Elisa's. Like Wolfgang Schwitter, he drove a convertible. His was a swanky black

22

Duesenberg with a white ragtop. I adored that car, though the Myrers would never own one like it. My father said if one of them ever rolled over, you were a goner.

"*Vater* is not exactly a farmer," said Elisa. "He is a professor. He's Herr Doktor Heinz Stadler, a name that means nothing on this side and everything on the other."

"How can he be a professor farmer?"

"*Vater* teaches new ideas in agriculture to graduate students. He's here to study hydroponics at your Cornell University."

"The last thing he looks like is a farmer," I said. I'd watched him a few times from my bedroom window. He always had a lighted cigarette hanging from his lips, and he walked briskly as though he had an important appointment.

"*Vater* comes only on weekends from the university," she said. Then she grabbed my arm to stop me. "What's that?"

"It sounds like a bugle." I looked at my watch. It was exactly nine thirty, the time the prison whistle blew signaling lights-out on The Hill. It was as much a part of the town as the lake was, as Joyland Park and Hoopes Park were. Weeknights during the school year, like a lot of kids playing outdoors, I had to start home when the whistle blew. Weekend nights curfew for me was eleven o'clock.

"Listen!" Elisa cried.

The bugler was playing taps.

I whispered the words to myself: ". . . from the lake, from the sky . . . safe-ly rest. . . ."

The bugler had begun another round. It came from the prison's loudspeakers.

We stood side by side listening, our shoulders hunched against the cold. In a few houses ahead of us on Genesee Street, people had come out to hear better, winter coats over their shoulders.

Who could help listening? Who anywhere had ever heard such a melancholy wailing?

"This is new, *ja*?" Elisa said when it was over.

"It's never happened before," I said. "I think it's the new man, the lifer who came in last week. Daddy said he plays bugle, trumpet, and cornet."

"The brass instruments, ha? What is a lifer?"

I told Elisa a lifer was a con who was locked up forever.

"And some are executed, yes?"

"Not here anymore. But we've had some very famous murderers. We had Rhubarb Boxer the first year we got here. He was famous for killing rich wives with rhubarb leaves. He ground them up and put them in salads. Rhubarb leaves are lethal! That's why you never see any leaves on rhubarb in stores."

"Aren't you afraid to have murderers so near?" she asked me.

"No. In fact sometimes the prisoners work down in our yard. Sometimes murderers. My father prefers them."

"Why?" Her eyes were popping out of her head.

"Because they're different from thieves and swindlers. Robbing and swindling are habitual behavior, so you have to watch yourself around their kind. But murder isn't a habit."

"I never thought of that," Elisa said. "I never knew about rhubarb leaves either."

"Eat a few and you'll croak in two weeks. No known cause of death."

She laughed and rolled her eyes. "Oh, the things you know!"

We began walking again, almost jogging, it was so cold. Those who had come outside to hear the bugler went back inside.

"My whole family are musicians," Elisa said. "All except me. But I love good music, as they do, and that was good music! Does this new lifer have a name?"

"I don't know it," I said, "and if I did, I wouldn't be able to tell you about him. My father has rules against discussing the prisoners with anyone."

"I don't want to be just anyone," Elisa said.

"Nobody does."

"So find out," she said. "Find out everything about him."

5

"HIS NAME IS Slater Carr," my father said. "All we need is another inmate! We're bursting at the seams as it is."

"Can't you tell the superintendent that?"

"I asked for him, Jess. I can't pass him up. The way he plays? It wouldn't be fair to The Blues."

There were more prisoners than ever before. It was because of the hard times. It was because people were driven to do desperate things. They had too many bills and too little money. Some, like Horace Joy, had lost everything, taking all the Joystep employees with him.

"Did Slater Carr kill someone?" I asked my father.

"He was involved in a planned robbery where the victim was shot to death. He was convicted at trial, though he didn't pull the trigger."

"Was it because of a woman? Was it what's called a crime of passion?"

My father said, "It was what's called a crime of stupidity.

He's just twenty, sweetheart. That young man has a God-given talent, and now the only way he can show it off is in a prison band."

"But I bet you're glad for the band's sake."

"I'd rather hear him playing at Carnegie Hall any day! He's ruined his life."

"There must have been a great love in his life who wanted expensive things like diamond rings and mink coats," I said.

"Don't spin one of your stories around this poor fellow. He's a sad sack, honey. All our inmates are, really."

My father hadn't liked it when I'd invented the idea that Bonnie and Clyde nicked their arms with a safety pin and pressed them together to commingle their blood. Then they said together, "Blood of my blood. Heart of my heart."

My father had said angrily, "Where did you hear that malarkey?"

"She makes things up!" Seth had said.

Sometimes I did make it up. Other times I got ideas from my mother's under-the-mattress library. Most of the books there had belonged to Rhubarb Boxer, the last inmate who was electrocuted at Cayuta Prison. Once he was executed, my father brought a box down from The Hill and told my mother to "do something with these." He couldn't have looked at them. He'd probably imagined my mother would give good books to a good cause, Catholic Charities or someplace like that.

Not those books! Those books weren't going anywhere. Those books had titles like *The Harem*, *Torment*, and *The Body's Rapture*. My mother kept them under her mattress, and from time to time I got one of them out, sneaked it back to my room, and read the purple prose wide-eyed, my heart banging.

Seth had always laughed at the "histories" I invented for the cons.

My father never called them cons. He called them inmates. He never called them by their first names. He called each one mister.

Some evenings when he walked down from The Hill and opened the front door, I was waiting there, as I'd been that night, hoping for news about the new arrival.

"That's enough about our bugle boy," Daddy said, after we'd talked awhile on the front steps. "Where's your mother?"

He was a big man, tall and stout. He had been Blocker Myrer, a star football player at the University of Alabama. He had wistful blue eyes that seemed some days to be remembering times his name was in headlines on the sports page and crowds stood to their feet and shouted, "Blocker! Blocker! Blocker!"

"Mother's in the music room," I said. "She's been

playing the same song over and over."

"Maybe she wants to get it perfect."

"'Ah! Sweet mystery of life at last I've found thee.'" I imitated my mother's soprano.

"'Ah! I know at last the secret of it all!'" my father sang back. He was chuckling. He thought it was as funny as I did: Olivia Myrer singing at her piano about the mystery of life.

But my mother could find mystery and intrigue inside a Post Toasties box. Olivia Myrer lived for gossip, dreamed of scandal she would know the insides and outsides of, and often in the evening stood in darkened rooms of our house, holding up one slat of the venetian blinds for a secret look at the neighbors' doings. I would have bet my life that was what she had been up to that night since she had stopped playing the Steinway.

"Daddy, is Slater Carr going to play taps every night?"

"Yes, I think so."

"What's he like?"

"He's a musician, that's all I know."

"Is he a Negro?"

"No, he's not a darkie. . . . I'm going to make your mother and me a nightcap. Do you want a Coke?"

"No, thanks." Before I left Elisa that night, she'd said, "Let's wave good night to each other at exactly midnight."

Meanwhile I planned to find Mugshot, the cat, and

take him up to my bedroom to listen to dance music on the radio.

I was too self-conscious to dance, but I knew all the popular songs word for word. So did Richard.

"Arthur?" Olivia Myrer called out. "Is that you?"

"I'm making us grasshoppers, honey."

"Did I actually hear a bugle playing earlier? I never heard anything like it!"

"I've got me a first-class bugler, Olivia."

"He made me sad," she called back. "I never felt like crying before when I heard taps."

On my way past the music room I stopped short, ducked my head in the door, and shouted, "Boo!"

My mother jumped away from the blind, holding her hand over her heart. "You scared me, Jess!"

"Who were you spying on, the Stadlers?"

"I wouldn't get your hopes up that you're going to be friends with the Stadler girl," my mother said, "just because she came over here to meet you."

"We already are friends, or why would she come here?"

"She was probably just snooping."

"Then why would she ask me to a movie, and why would we wave good night at midnight exactly?" I said.

My mother said, "We'll see how many other movies she invites you to and how many nights you wave to each other at midnight exactly. We'll see."

My father came into the music room with two green drinks in cocktail glasses.

"What'll we see?" he asked.

"Your daughter has dreams of becoming bosom pals with Miss Germany."

"Who said I wanted a bosom pal? What do you call Richard?"

"A boy isn't a bosom pal of a girl for obvious reasons," my mother said. She took a sip of the grasshopper and smiled at my father. "Thank you, dearest."

"You're welcome. . . . Why wouldn't Jessie become good friends with Miss Germany?"

"Because the mother thinks she's better than anyone else."

"She's just aloof," I said. "She's not gregarious."

"Where'd you learn that word?" my father asked.

"Her sidekick taught it to her," said my mother. She looked at me and said, "Richard Nolan. Right?"

"Wrong," I lied. "Elisa Stadler."

"I bet you haven't met the mother," my mother said.

"Not yet."

"Don't hold your breath while you're waiting. I'll bet you never get inside that house either."

"Who cares?" I said.

"Miss Germany waltzes into this house as if she owned it, but I very much doubt you'll get a return invitation."

"Maybe I don't want one," I said.

"Mrs. Stadler is not just aloof! She has no manners. And she's a renter, so how dare she put on airs! Who knows what her background is!"

"Olivia, don't talk that way," my father said. "We have to live in this town."

"I have to. You don't. You live up on The Hill."

"But I'm always thinking of you, sweetheart. Always."

"Pfffft!" My mother tried hard not to smile. She enjoyed my father's teasing her, but she pretended not to notice it. She pursed her small lips and ran a hand through her wiry red hair. She was such a little woman to have hooked this huge husband with hands like a bear, towering over her.

"Let me tell you what the mother had to say to me one day in the aisle of Holy Family," said my mother. "I said to her that since we are new neighbors, we should get to know each other. Then I said, 'Do you want to stop by the house now? Now is as good a time as any.' She said, 'Oh, I cannot. My husband is waiting outside.' And I said, 'Bring him. Of course I want to meet Mr. Stadler.'"

My father said, "She said, 'Herr Stadler and I have very little time together. Not enough time for neighbors, I fear.'"

My father and I had heard that story three or four times. He said, "Ollie, maybe it's as simple as that. They prefer their own company."

"No, Arthur, she was incinerating something. What I don't know." I knew the word she meant to say was *insinuating*, and of course the warden did too.

My father was always amused by her malapropisms. He said, "You don't know what she was incinerating, but it burns you up."

My mother didn't get it. She never got it.

"You're exactly right, Arthur. It burns me up!"

Seth was a mama's boy, and he didn't like it when our father made fun of her without her knowing it. Seth would cuss out the warden behind his back. At seventeen Seth was going through a stage where he was angry with our father most of the time.

My father said it was a natural stage.

He said Seth was just jockeying for position in a house of two males.

"You never let him win, though," my mother said. She always let Seth win.

"It's just a game, Ollie. All fathers and sons play it."

"It isn't a game to Seth," she said.

"Oh, I don't take it seriously."

He didn't either. What my father took seriously was

what went on up on The Hill.

What my father took really really seriously was the Bands Behind Bars Annual Award, known as the Black Baaa.

Last year he had lost again to The Louisiana Stripes, a band from New Orleans.

6

SLATER CARR

IN COASTAL GEORGIA if you seemed crazy or you did something crazy, you were liable to hear someone tell you, "You belong in Peachy!"

It was the Peachy Insane Asylum, where Slater Carr had been born. He really did belong in Peachy for most of his life—not in the mental institution but farther down the road, in an asylum of another kind, the Peachy Orphan Asylum.

Whether you were from PIA or POA, Peachies knew.

Peachies knew which place you were from too.

The insanes sometimes got out for supervised walks, and that was a sight and a half, some of them drooling, their eyes wandering around the sockets, some of them mumbling, screeching, sticking their tongues out not at anything.

Times they ambled around Peachy, people rocked on their porches, shaking their heads—those who didn't go inside and hook the screen doors. Some wrote to *The Peachy Banner* complaining, "Let them stay on the asylum grounds! We don't want the loonies loose."

The orphans were another story. Peachies would call them "poor things." Christmastime Peachies gave them old clothes cleaned and pressed to look like new and stockings filled with candy and fruit. The ladies of the Peachy Baptist Church wrapped one toy for each orphan in Christmas paper. POAs went to Peachy schools and anywhere anyone else in Peachy went, except for nighttime, when they stayed in the asylum from six P.M. to six A.M.

The favorite punishment for wrongdoing at POA was an old-fashioned one: Anyone who misbehaved was locked inside the closet next to the headmistress's office.

Slater could not stand being shut up in there. He would scratch himself until he bled. He would shiver and cry and call out for God to help him. He had never known fear like that, nor could he ever predict the offense that would land him there: playing his harmonica after night bell, holding a mirror under the downstairs steps to see up girls' dresses, sleeping in church.

When he first heard of The Hole, notorious in prison gossip even before he was taken off to Cayuta, he made sure to include it when he wrote the required account of his crime. He wanted it written on his records: *claustrophobic.*

7

Since our arrival in Cayuta, my father had ruled over The Hill like a benevolent dictator. He was strict but not cruel or unfair. On Citizens' Day, for the first time, Cayutians over twenty-one saw for themselves what went on inside the walls. They saw the workshops, which turned out the state license plates, the laundry, the library, the kitchen and dining room, and most of the men serving time there.

My father had thought up Citizens' Day to make it possible for him to get The Blues included in certain public holiday celebrations. It was fair to say his major preoccupation was with this band. It had come in second two years in a row. There was one prison band from New Orleans that nearly always won the Baaa, but Daddy told me that was because it was all Negro. He believed Negroes were known for a superior sense of rhythm.

That Louisiana band used trick steps and to my father's way of thinking were more performers than musicians.

Anyone who heard Slater Carr would know the difference, my father told me. Mr. Carr needed no frills or gimmicks, he said.

He sent shivers down your spine just doing what he did, just blowing that horn, he said.

Daddy talked a lot about this new man. His name would come into conversation a surprising number of times when he was with me.

"I'll tell you one thing about Mr. Carr, Jessie. He's claustrophobic. That's underlined three times on his profile."

"Then how can he stand to be locked up in his cell from four-thirty in the afternoon until seven-thirty A.M.?"

"I worry about that a lot, sweetheart."

"You really like him, don't you?"

"I was never a young man of talent, Jessie. I guess we Myrers aren't blessed that way. Your grandfather is a dentist. Your brother follows after me with football skills. But Seth has never said anything about what he wants to do when he's through school. I don't think he knows or cares. This kid is different. He lives for his music. I got a little radio for him."

"You always spoil the murderers, Daddy."

"Mr. Carr is an accomplice to murder, Jessie. The ones I spoil are the ones I don't think got a fair shake."

"Remember when you gave Rhubarb Boxer some away time and he stole a hundred dollars from Crazy Carl Plum?"

"I never believed the Plums. Carl is no angel, but they treat him like one. He can't do anything wrong, just because he's not all there. . . . Rhubarb Boxer didn't deserve The Hole."

"I hope Slater Carr never does something to land in The Hole, if he's claustrophobic."

"I wish we could get rid of that thing," my father said. "No one can say I haven't tried."

Anyone, everyone in Cayuta Prison feared going to that underground chamber below the basement. My father said there was not an inmate on The Hill who hadn't heard about it. It was fifty feet long, a dark, stinking cave lined with cells made out of solid rock and sealed with iron doors. The cells were bare. There was no sink, no toilet, and no bed. The only place to sit or lie down on was the dank cement floor. The only food was a single meal each day, a watery stew without meat, only a few carrots and potatoes. A paper cup of lukewarm water with it.

Silence was the rule in The Hole. Complainers were lashed. Any who whimpered or groaned were punished with fumes of lime wetted down with water.

I said, "Well, Daddy, at least you got rid of the electric chair."

"I didn't do that, honey. That's gone thanks to Reinhardt Schwitter. He knows how to manipulate the city planners and our board. He made them aware of how bad we looked to visitors when we put a man to death. He also mentioned the dreadful drain on electricity."

"I'm surprised Mr. Schwitter cared."

"Nobody liked all the lights in the house blinking every time someone from The Hill was electrocuted. Schwitter had the clout to stop it."

8

CONTRARY TO MY mother's prediction, Elisa and I became fast friends. Richard complained to me at first, telling me that he felt abandoned, particularly at lunchtime, when the sharks circled the High East cafeteria. I invited him to join Elisa and me, but he said he didn't want to be a third wheel, and the funny thing was I was glad. He was my very best buddy, but there was a difference between hanging out with a boy and having a girl friend.

Elisa and I ate lunch together in the cafeteria and walked to and from school. That established us in everyone's eyes as what my mother'd call bosom pals. I sometimes looked around to see if J. J. Joy was watching and if she was still of the opinion I should have been at West.

Since we could see into each other's bedrooms, sometimes Elisa would put a record on her windup Victrola and play some big hit of the day for me. She said she'd done it before we'd become friends, just to see if I would look out at her.

"Why me?" I said.

"Because of Seth," she said. "I wanted to meet Seth."

"Well, at least you're honest," I told her. "I looked out, but I hid behind the curtain."

"I knew you were there." She chuckled. "I wanted to meet you both, you and Seth."

"So what do you think of Seth?"

"I met him only that one time when he was leaving as I was arriving. He hardly spoke."

"He's not used to girls," I said.

"What a waste! He looks like such a heartbreaker."

"He's got the name without the game."

Elisa loved languages and, besides German and English, could speak Spanish fluently and some French as well.

She could sing all the words to "What a Difference a Day Makes" in Spanish. She would stand at her bedroom window and croon, "*Cuando vuelva a tu lado.*"

"I think of the difference the day we met made in my life," Elisa said. She was helping me put into Seth's crime scrapbook the news of John Dillinger's escape, that past March, from the Crown Point, Indiana, jail. Seth was an Indian giver, so I knew he'd want the scrapbook back one day, which was okay with me. He was the big gangster fan. I didn't mind keeping the scrapbook up-to-date for him. Whatever it was he was going through was making him miserable.

Elisa had made a paste from flour and water in our kitchen. She said, "I have never had a close friend, because we move so much. I was always too full of bash. And too ashamed of my accent."

"There's no such word as *bash*. Just say bashful. If I had your accent, I'd never shut my mouth."

"You don't much now," Elisa teased. "I was so tired of my hobbies: looking at stars through my binoculars, pasting stamps in my stamp book. I will always remember the first time I saw your John Dillinger poster up in your bedroom. You said he was so sharp, which was an English slang I didn't know. Then when we went to the movies, you would not say Lew Ayres was better-looking. You are so stubborn, Jessica!"

"Lew Ayres is a close second. But Lew Ayres would never have the brains to escape from prison with a pistol whittled from the top of a wooden washboard. Next John blackened it with shoe polish. Since then, the heat has been off Pretty Boy Floyd." I told her what my father had told me about the jailbreak, adding, "They're all out to get John again."

"Why are all your gangsters handsome or pretty?" Elisa asked.

"Those are just their nicknames," I explained. "Most aren't that complimentary. There's Bugsy and Bugs, Legs and Machine Gun Kelly. A lot of them have acne scars on their faces. A lot of them are really homely, Elisa."

"My mother says in her opinion you glamorize criminals in this country." Elisa continued. "You give them nicknames, as though they were your pets."

Elisa ran her hands under water to wash off the paste she'd made.

"Don't your criminals have nicknames?" I asked.

"I do not remember a single criminal. Neither does my mother. In Germany we never feature them, as you do here. Even your own maid is a criminal with a nickname. Myra from Elmira."

"No, that's just what I call Myra. She's no criminal. She's in the Elmira Reformatory because she got pregnant when she was thirteen."

"Is that all she did? Got pregnant?"

"See, she was an orphan and some older boy at the orphanage got her pregnant."

"That's enough to get sent to a reformatory?"

"If you're an orphan, it's enough. She didn't have any money to bribe the judge either."

"Why would your mother hire her to work for you?"

"She works for us because we don't have to pay her anything. Employees of the penal system get maids from Elmira Reformatory for nothing. It's a courtesy."

"Speaking of free help, are you going to tell me what

you found out about Slater Carr? If he's a lifer, he must have done something really bad."

"How many times do I have to tell you I can't discuss him with anyone?" I said.

"I told you I don't want to be just anyone." She was grinning as though she knew me better than that.

"Okay then," I said. "What I'm going to tell you has to stay between us. Say, 'I swear!'"

"I swear!"

"Okay." I slammed the scrapbook shut and faced Elisa across the kitchen table. "Slater Carr killed the man who took his sweetheart from him. My father said, 'Think of it, Jessie. All because of one great, powerful love of a woman, he is now behind bars for life.'"

It was not something my father would ever say.

The warden would never romanticize a crime of passion, which I believed he scorned because he was not a passionate man. Sentimental but not passionate. Daddy would maybe be sympathetic with a man committing a crime to feed his family or accidentally killing someone in a fight that got out of control.

"Ach!" Elisa exclaimed. "He killed the man who took away his woman." Now her eyes were wide and excited.

I loved making up stories. Both Seth and Richard would find me out and protest, "You made that up!" but I could see that Elisa believed every word. Maybe it was the only way

I was superior to her. I could make her believe me.

I had just finished one of Olivia Myrer's under-the-mattress books called *Union Square*, by Albert Halper. A shy and idealistic man had burst into his dream girl's house to save her from a fire, and with her was a man, naked as she was.

The rest of the story was solely mine.

"That was when he riddled the other man with bullets," I continued. "Then he reloaded his pistol, preparing to riddle her with bullets too, but she said, 'Oh, love, forgive me.' He threw down the pistol and embraced her, his one and only love."

"I would never forgive that *Hure*!" Elisa said.

"Well, he loved her."

"And she was in bed with a nobody?"

"He wasn't a nobody, see. He was the sheriff's son."

"I only blame her," Elisa said. "That *Sau*! You tell me so much about life, Jessica."

"I do?"

"Always," Elisa said. "Thank you for telling me about Slater Carr. Will he take John Dillinger's place now in your heart?"

I had never thought of Dillinger's having a place in my heart, but neither had I ever seen Elisa that excited about anything. I told her that before Slater Carr took Dillinger's place in my heart, I had to see him.

I had never yet seen a handsome man from The Hill. The ones I watched from the window, clipping our hedges or shoveling our sidewalks, seemed to have big noses, pimples on their faces, or big bellies from the starch and grease in the prison diet. My father liked to tease my mother and me: "Do you think I'm going to send the good-looking ones down to you two?"

"*Pfffft*," my mother would answer, hiding her smile behind her hand.

9

SLATER CARR

Miss Purrington started him on the drums because that was what every little kid at Peachy wanted to play. Next she taught him the trumpet. He'd learn by playing hymns like "Nearer My God to Thee."

His favorite hymn became "Lord, I'm Coming Home":

> I've wasted many precious years,
> Now I'm coming home;
> I now repent with bitter tears;
> Lord, I'm coming home.

"You, Slater," she shouted up at the band, "read what's written under the title of that hymn, in little letters on the left."

"William J. Kirkpatrick," he answered.

"Not the name of the composer! Read his directions!"

"With feeling."

"So? Where's the feeling? Play that with feeling!"

"I don't feel anything because I haven't had any precious years to waste."

"Then practice for the future, Slater Carr. Someday you'll know what the words mean: I'm coming home. Say them to me."

"I'm coming home."

"Now say it on your trumpet. Say, 'Lord, I'm Coming Home!'"

10

ELISA AND I were as unalike as grapes and walnuts. Elisa was affectionate, calling me *Süsse* and always reminding me how glad of our friendship she was. I was my mother's daughter, as demonstrative as a stone. Close as I could come to showing her my feelings was sometimes calling Elisa dear heart, in a teasing tone.

She was the only person in my life who called me Jessica. She had told me that I wasn't a Jessica at all, but I should always call myself that. "When the person becomes dear, then the name does too," she said.

She had talked me into letting my hair grow longer. I drew the line at manicures.

"All right, but I wish you would stop biting your nails, Jessica. I love to give manicures. One day perhaps I may become a manicurist." She was always saying what she would perhaps become: a teacher, a rich man's wife, a translator, a poet.

Elisa loved poetry, one American poet especially, named Sara Teasdale.

"Never heard of her," I'd said. I hadn't heard of her because I didn't read poetry, except for the Burma Shave ads along the road:

> **THE ANSWER TO**
>> **A MAIDEN'S PRAYER**
>>> **IS NOT A CHIN**
>>>> **OF STUBBY HAIR**
>>>>> **Burma-Shave**

One day Elisa said, "Listen to what Sara Teasdale wrote.

"*TO E.*

"*I have remembered beauty in the night,*
Against black silences I waked to see
A shower of sunlight over Italy
And green Ravello dreaming on her height;
I have remembered music in the dark,
The clean swift brightness of a fugue of Bach's,
And running water singing on the rocks
When once in English woods I heard a lark.

"*But all remembered beauty is no more*
Than a vague prelude to the thought of you—

You are the rarest soul I ever knew,
Lover of beauty, knightliest and best;
My thoughts seek you as waves that seek the shore,
And when I think of you, I am at rest.

"That's how I want to feel someday about someone," Elisa said.

"I like poetry better when someone reads it," I said.

"Don't you want to feel that way about someone someday?"

"I have to think about that."

"What is there to think about?"

"Nothing. Everything. I'm just getting used to talking about ideas that usually stay in my head. Sometimes I don't even know they're there. Then something makes me see them."

"Sara Teasdale killed herself," Elisa said.

"She did not."

"She did too."

"Daddy told me if anyone thinking about suicide could shut his eyes and see how he would turn out if he stayed alive, no one would ever do it."

"Oh, I believe that too. And I believe a lot of people have suicidal thoughts," Elisa said. "Why do you blush?"

"I've thought of doing it. Sort of." I was expecting a reaction, a cry of No!, wide eyes, at least a raised eyebrow.

"Sort of? I've thought of jumping! Every time we went somewhere high, like the Eiffel Tower. You know, in Paris? I'd look down and say to myself, 'Jump, Elisa!'"

"I know the Eiffel Tower is in Paris. I might not go places, but I know about them!"

"Jumping, drowning, shooting yourself if you can find a gun," said Elisa. "I think anyone in her right mind thinks about doing it at some point. I believe we all have inside lives as well as outside ones. Sometimes the inside life takes over."

"Is that what happened to Sara Teasdale?"

"Maybe. Or maybe she believed something about her life was worse than it really was."

"She probably had dark thoughts," I said.

"I used to have dark thoughts," she said.

"About what?"

"About never belonging anywhere, missing Germany, never having a real home."

"You had a life instead."

"I didn't have friends until you. I never even petted a cat the way I pet your Mugshot. I still hardly ever see my father, and he is the most important person in my life. . . . What are your dark thoughts about?"

"I miss Elmira, New York."

"What do you miss about it?"

"Myself. I was myself there. When we moved here, we

53

found out all the prison kids went to Cayuta High West. I think they didn't want us at East."

"I don't have such dark thoughts since I met you," said Elisa.

"Me neither since you waltzed across the street."

11

A GOOD MANY Cayutians had summer homes on the lake. They lived there from Memorial Day to Labor Day. Some places were shacks, unheated, with outdoor plumbing, and others were grander. Our family could never move there summers because my father had to be in his home at the bottom of Retribution Hill, on call if anything went wrong at the prison.

We could look up and see the prison and hear it. There were shouts from the yard where men recreated. There was always a band rehearsal and the sound of individual band members practicing the drums or the saxophone—whatever instruments they played. Those times prisoners cut our lawn or put on the storm windows, I wasn't allowed to talk to them or even appear when they were there.

This warm day in the middle of June, Elisa and I were at my house, making egg-and-olive sandwiches for a picnic. Elisa had brought the bread and olives across the street while I hard-boiled the eggs. I had made a batch of chocolate nut fudge, a treat Elisa liked.

Many of our classmates had moved to Cayuta Lake for the summer with their families. I remembered past summers I'd skulked around feeling sorry for myself. I had the idea not going to the lake summers was just another way of not being part of things. I wasn't part of things anyway, but I used to think maybe going to the lake could change that.

Now Elisa and I reveled in the idea we had the neighborhood and Hoopes Park to ourselves.

The Stadlers were renting the Sontag house indefinitely, paying twenty dollars a month. Tom Sontag had taken a job as a bull, hired by the railroads to toss off hoboes. Gertie Sontag had been living all winter in their summer camp, which had coal heat and no indoor plumbing. The Sontags were in bad shape, since Tom Sontag had worked for years at Joystep Shoes. Now he was doing work he was ashamed of, often hurting badly the men he threw from the trains.

Whenever Elisa came over to our house, she would wear things that matched perfectly and white things that were beyond white, they were so clean and pressed. She always wore her grandmother's small gold dachshund pin. Her nails were never chipped. She had her own favorite

American perfume too. Evening in Paris. She said she just liked the name. "Someday," she said to me, "we will go together on a visit to Paris, high up in the Eiffel Tower." She said there was an outside elevator. "You go up at a slant," she said.

"Not me," I said. "I won't go up in anything that's at a slant."

"You will get over it for Paris!"

"Not even for Paris. *Pas du tout!*" I was trying out what little French I knew. I liked the idea of dropping a foreign word into a sentence as Elisa did.

We were always laughing and squealing, and that morning my mother came from reading *Picture Show* on the sun porch and stood in the kitchen doorway, watching us. She had on one of her flowery silk housecoats, her auburn hair pulled back behind her head and held with a white ribbon.

I was embarrassed by my mother's reading material. Never mind the books under her mattress. Even though I read them, I believed that my real reading material—the bestsellers sent from book clubs, and the novels I checked out of the library—made up for my dips into my mother's trash.

On rare occasions I'd seen Elisa's mother in the library, although Mrs. Stadler darted from view when she saw me.

I asked the librarian what kinds of books she read, and I was told that she was learning English by reading the poet T. S. Eliot.

Elisa looked up from the sandwiches we were making and said, "I didn't see you standing there, Mrs. Myrer."

"How are you, Elisa, and how is your family? In all this time your mother and your father have not come across to visit."

Elisa skipped past that comment by saying, "My mother wonders why you feed the tramps."

"I didn't think your mother had any curiosity about us."

"Your tramps come to our house."

"They aren't our tramps. We don't own them!" I said. "We always erase the chalk marks they make in front of our house, so other tramps don't know we give handouts."

"Then there must be a grape vineyard," said Elisa, "because tramps are in the neighborhood."

"She means a grapevine," I told my mother.

Elisa said, "My mother says, 'Who knows what kind of people they are?'"

"They are people down on their luck," said my mother.

"They're not just in our neighborhood. I saw one up in Hoopes Park last week," I said.

I'd almost forgotten that there was this tramp shuffling along in clothes too big, out of place in the rock garden, where I liked to go. At first I thought it was Crazy Carl Plum, the backward son of the town funeral director who played jacks sometimes in the garden. But this man had a small, long brown dog with him he led on a piece of rope. I had never seen such a skinny, undernourished creature.

The tramp must have come from Railroad Woods, near the tracks, where Richard said there was a hobo camp. Last winter he took gloves and scarves to them, and leftovers from the Nolan refrigerator.

I'd called after the tramp, "Don't you feed your dog?"

"Mind your beeswax!" he'd shouted back. Then he'd dragged the poor dog across the gravel, muttering at him, "Come on, you stupid animal!"

If I had told my mother about the way he'd treated the dog, she would have marched to that spot instantly and stayed there, hoping to catch this man. She would have scolded him, shaking a finger at him, telling him she would report him to the SPCA if he didn't take better care of his dog. That was one thing I liked about her. She stuck up for cats, dogs, birds. She wouldn't even kill a spider in our house.

Another thing about my mother I liked was the way she treated Myra from Elmira. Sometimes I'd see Myra waiting for the bus back to Elmira, wearing Mother's worn-out sling pumps with bobby socks, or sporting on a sweater some five-and-dime rhinestone pin Mother had tired of, which Myra wore scrubbing floors. Working alongside each other hanging clothes or doing dishes, they gossiped together about Hollywood stars, and my mother occasionally invited her into the backyard on summer afternoons for a glass of iced tea.

"Poor Myra!" said my mother once. "That's what happens when you give your most valuable possession away to some sweet-talker. No one buys the cow when they can get the milk free."

"Was Daddy a sweet-talker?" I asked her.

She waved her hand at me as though she were waving away flies.

My mother wasn't up for many heart-to-heart talks about the facts of life. If I'd listened only to her, I'd still think babies came from long-legged large white wading birds with red beaks.

My mother finished the discussion about tramps by asking Elisa, "Hasn't your mother ever known someone who's down on his luck? We're in the middle of a depression, in case she doesn't know that."

Elisa said, "My mother says Americans encourage lawbreakers with their movies."

"We're not talking about lawbreakers," said my mother. "We're talking about homeless people. . . . Are those eggs from our refrigerator?"

"Yes," I said.

"Surprise, surprise," said my mother.

"Elisa brought the bread and olives."

"And the lettuce and the mayonnaise," said Elisa.

I knew my mother thought Elisa was using me.

One day I asked my mother what I could possibly have that Elisa would want. She had an answer without even thinking about it. "Someday ask yourself what a bright, attractive girl is doing with someone younger and from people she deems not good enough to introduce to her own family. Maybe the answer to that is someone likes being superior to someone else. Someone likes to lord it over someone else."

"I tell her things about people. That's what she likes."

"*Pffft*. What do you know about people?"

But that morning Mother had something up her sleeve, because she had that certain sugary tone to her voice. "Where are you going for your picnic, girls?"

"The backyard," I said.

My mother looked at Elisa with one of her crooked smiles and said, "Oh, is the picnic in your backyard, Elisa?"

"Not over there," said Elisa. "This yard."

"I am afraid that's not possible," my mother said.

"We always picnic here," I said, though this was to be only our second picnic.

"Not today! You know how your father feels about your being anywhere near one of the prisoners," said my mother.

Elisa's eyes grew large with excitement, and she said something in German I'd heard her exclaim before. She was probably cussing. Sometimes German wasn't that far from English, and I understood: words like *Hure* and *Sau* and *mein Gott*.

"Is there a prisoner coming?" she asked.

"There is a prisoner already here," my mother answered. "The Bugle Boy."

Elisa ran to the window near the dinette. "Can I see him?"

"You're not supposed to see him. He's cleaning out the shed with my husband."

I said, "How come Daddy let him be off grounds so soon? I thought an inmate wasn't supposed to get any away time until he'd been here a year."

"If you ask me, rules don't apply to that boy," said my mother. "Daddy lets him get away with murder."

Elisa and I giggled at that, and my mother got red. "You know what I mean. He's Daddy's pet."

Elisa was at the window. "Jessica . . . I see him! I see him."

I followed her to the dinette window.

"Look!" Elisa said. "The prisoner's playing with the stray cat."

"The prisoner loves that little stray," said Mother. "I've looked out to see him holding it and talking to it like it was a baby. You girls come away from there now."

Elisa and I couldn't see the prisoner's face well. He was wearing the blue cap with the white *B* on it. Only band members had the *B* on their caps. He had the peak pulled down over his eyes. We just had a side view of him. He looked very thin and young. He looked like a kid.

My father was sitting on the wooden garden bench while Slater Carr stood talking to him. The kitten was rubbing its face against the prisoner's pants leg.

"We have to call the SPCA to come for the kitty," my mother said, getting to her feet. "I'll see if I can capture it."

She started out the kitchen door, saying over her shoulder, "You girls stay put! You're not even supposed to look at anyone from The Hill."

That was the moment the small wire-haired brown dog appeared, running at the kitten, which headed for the nearest tree. I ran out to stop the dog, and Elisa followed.

My mother turned around and held up both hands, like a traffic cop rerouting cars. "Go back!" she shouted at Elisa and me.

"My heart beats rapidly," said Elisa. "We almost saw Slater."

"I thought you didn't fancy criminals."

"You have made Slater intriguing to me," said Elisa, "and he's a musician too. He killed only one person, Jessica."

"Most of our murderers killed just one." I'd never told her Slater was an accomplice, not a murderer. I figured my story of a crime of passion was more intriguing than the truth, and the truth wouldn't change anything now.

"But Dillinger killed more than one," she answered.

"He's different. He's a bank robber."

"I think Slater would be better for you to think about than John Dillinger."

"*You* think about him," I said. "I give him to you."

A time would come when I would remember saying that to Elisa and regretting it with all my heart.

12

SLATER CARR

At first Warden Myrer and the prisoner didn't talk, just smoked and looked around at the town, or the lake if Carr was doing away work up there, wherever he was, because Myrer had started picking him up to take him back to The Hill.

Eventually they talked some, mostly about music. Except for Miss Purr of Peachy, Georgia, Carr didn't know anyone who knew that much about bands and good songs for them to play. After the warden heard that the prisoner could sing, he'd say Carr should do that, too, when The Blues were performing. He'd keep after him. "What song do you like, Mr. Carr?"

"'Till Times Get Better.'"

"I don't know that one."

"It's a song Jabbo Smith sings."

"I never heard of him, either."

"Because I'm making it hard for you. He's out of Georgia. Did you ever hear of Roy Eldridge?"

"The trumpeter. Sure."

"Jabbo Smith bested him in a cut session. That's how good he is."

Silence for a while, and then the warden said, "One thing I like."

"What?"

"Relaxing like this. Talking about music. I never talk with anyone about it."

"You got kids?"

"Neither of them cares about it. My wife does, sort of, but her musical knowledge doesn't go that deep."

"Jabbo Smith is like me," Slater Carr said.

"How come?"

"We were both born on Christmas Eve. He's a southerner from Georgia, same as me, and he was brought up in an orphanage too. Did you ever hear of The Jenkins Orphanage Band?"

"Oh, sure. A Reverend Daniel Jenkins started a band called The Pick-a-Ninny, way back. A famous band. How'd you hear about them?"

"I heard of them from a lady at the Peachy Orphan Asylum. Her ambition is to do something similar. She started a band called The Georgia Peaches. I played in it when I was back there."

"Well, she'll probably never do anything as good, because The Jenkins Band was all Negroes," said the warden. "They used to play on the streets of Charleston, South Carolina."

"Miss Purr always says that's a myth about the colored playing music better than us."

"I'd like to believe it's a myth, Mr. Carr."

"Why's that, boss?"

"That's what we've got for competition, Mr. Carr. That's what The Blues are up against every year. Negroes. To make matters worse, these boys are from New Orleans."

"Why is that worse?"

"Down in New Orleans it's all music. You hear it everywhere."

"I bet we can do it!" said Slater Carr. "I bet we can lick them!"

"I dream of one day having that big Baaa on my desk," the warden told him. "You know they give out little Baaas for the band."

"It's something to shoot for," Slater said. Then he corrected it to "Aim for. It's something to aim for."

13

Elisa took the kitten.

"It was *Papachen* who said I could have it, but remember something: If you should ever meet my father, you must never tell how the prisoner loved the cat."

"If I ever meet him," I said.

"He has no time, Jessica. . . . The Sontags had mice in the basement, which helped convince Papa to let me have her," Elisa continued. "I name her Marlene, after my mother's favorite film star. Then maybe she will not care that this kitty lives with us."

"There's no movie star named Marlene."

"Marlene Dietrich. She is a German, but now she's in your Hollywood. Someday you'll see this kitty's namesake in the films. My mother believes she resembles Marlene, so she will like her named that too."

"The only Marlene in our town is Mayonnaise Marlene,

who's a telephone operator. Call her Dietrich instead."

Mostly white with one black ear and a black paw, Dietrich was at the Sontags'. Elisa said the cat liked to snooze inside a straw sailor hat belonging to Sophie Stadler.

It was a Friday night, and we had gone over to Hoopes Park to catch pollywogs for an aquarium we were starting. Mr. Stadler came back from Cornell on Friday nights, and Elisa said she had to get out of the house then.

"Why? I thought you liked your father."

We were sitting on one of the pale-green park benches, in front of the rose gardens with their heady perfume. We were throwing bread crumbs to the swans. The pollywogs we had collected could not be seen swimming in the murky water inside a Chase & Sanborn coffee can with holes punched in the top. The park lights had just come on, so we knew it was nine o'clock.

"Of course I like my own father," said Elisa. "I love him. But I have to give them time to be intimate."

I winced. "Don't talk about it. I don't even want to think about parents doing it. Thank Gawd mine don't do it."

"How did you get here, then, if they don't do it?"

"They did it twice. Once for Seth. The second time for me."

"Married people do it all the time."

A major mystery to me at that point in my life happened to be how I got there. Never mind the long-legged large white wading bird with the red beak; I wondered if my parents could have summoned forth stand-ins to go through the motions that produced children. My father had built a sleeping porch for himself and Seth. Once, when I asked my mother why most of my classmates' parents slept in the same bedroom, my mother shot back: "That's because they can't afford a bigger house."

"Your parents must be intimate, Jessica."

"No. They don't even sleep in the same room."

"Are they estranged?" Elisa asked.

"No. They get along just fine. He often comes home early to take a walk with her. Then he makes her grasshopper cocktails."

"I believe they do it secretly," Elisa said. "Even if it's *alle Jubeljahre einmal.* That's how we say once in a blue moon."

"Why would they do it secretly? They're married."

"They might not want you to know they do it."

"I'd just as soon not know," I said, "although I do know they don't do it. . . . Can't your father wait until they go to bed?"

"My *Mutti* prepares hors d'oeuvres for *Vater*, and they

have wine," said Elisa. "Remember, he has been gone all week."

I liked to watch the Stadlers on their front porch weekend nights he was home. I'd seen Heinz Stadler light two cigarettes at the same time and pass one to Mrs. Stadler. Mrs. Stadler put it into a long cigarette holder, which she held between two fingers. He sat with his arm around her and looked as if he were whispering sexy things to her.

One night my mother had moved away from the venetian blinds muttering, "I wouldn't let a man maul me right in plain view of the neighbors."

"Where would you let a man maul you?" I asked her.

She acted as though she hadn't heard me.

Elisa said, "Jessica, tell me something honestly. Is Seth never home because I'm there so much?"

"He started staying away from home before you moved across the street," I said. "Why do you always think about boys? I can take them or leave them."

"You are not German, that's why. We even have a word for the fear we'll be left behind when we're twenty-one, with everyone else married. *Torschlusspanik.* I love our language more than any other. We have a word for everything. One word for something it takes six words to describe in other languages. I miss so Potsdam, where I'm from." Elisa picked up the coffee can with our pollywogs in it. She said, "We'd better go. It's getting dark. . . . I think so much of whom I will marry someday. He will be my *Verlobter* first. My fiancé. My mother is always saying who would be a good *Verlobter* for me. The answer is someone like *Vater*. I want to marry a man like my father."

"I want to marry one like mine but with a different job."

"I want mine to be an idealist, and romantic."

"I wonder if my father is romantic," I said. "He couldn't be that romantic married to her. He's too involved with the prison anyway. Hey, I saw a note from Slater Carr to my father. You want to know what it said?"

"Of course! Why didn't you tell me before?"

"I was saving it to tell you. The note said, 'Boss, I have learned a special song for you, and I am ready to sing it. Yours truly, Mr. Carr.'"

"What song?"

"Search me. But I think I know why he learned it. I have a surprise for you."

We would often save surprises until we felt it was just the right time.

I said, "Slater Carr learned that song for the Fourth of July, I bet. The Blues are playing right in this very park on the Fourth. We can see Slater Carr plainly, up on the bandstand."

"Can we talk to him?"

"No one can talk to any of them."

"Someday perhaps I will marry a musician. . . . Oh, Jessica, listen!"

"What?"

"He's playing," Elisa whispered.

When Taps was over, Elisa said, "Jessica, one of us should fall in love. Then the other one can help her through it. From what I know of the subject, it is filled with pitfalls."

"*You* fall in love then. I don't feel like it."

"Don't make a comedy of it. I am telling you something more serious than our usual topics."

"I'm sorry. Don't fall for Seth, because he's undersexed."

"Who said?"

"I said. Coming from the kind of parents we have, where there is no action to speak of in the master bedroom, *ever*, how would he turn out? Undersexed."

"Are you undersexed too?"

"I must be. I never think about it."

"I hope that's not true for your sake, *Süsse*. I think it is important to want a man. I can't say want a boy. I don't want a boy."

"Who do you want?"

"If I could choose anyone we both know?"

"I hope you're not going to say Slater Carr."

"I like what you have told me about him."

"You do? What did I tell you about him that you like?"

Elisa grinned. "I like that he's a hothead when it comes to love."

"And that he murdered someone because of it?"

"There's the rub, as Mr. Shakespeare would say."

"As anyone would say."

"So I pick someone we both know. We both don't know many sharp boys. So it would have to be Wolfgang Schwitter."

"You hardly spoke two words to him, Phyllis."

"I know he called me Phyllis. But he didn't know me. He didn't know his father got us tickets. Hundreds of girls must speak to him—he's dark and handsome."

"Tall, dark, and handsome," I said. "Lots of luck."

"Thank you," Elisa said, not understanding the sarcasm.

Our conversation was suddenly halted by the sight of a swan swooping down on the same little brown dog that had chased Dietrich up a tree. The dog was swimming hard toward the swan. Its owner was wading in after it, waving a stick.

"I can't watch this," Elisa said. "He's going to beat that dog."

"Hey, you!" I shouted. "Leave him alone!"

The man paid no attention. He caught the dog by its collar and began beating it as the dog yelped. Both Elisa and I ran down to the water, shouting at the man to stop.

He cursed at us and disappeared into the woods near the park, the dog under his arm.

"We have to do something!" I said. "There must be something we can do for that poor scruffy dog."

"Poor Scruffy," said Elisa. "We have to get Richard. He can find a way to rescue the dog."

"Maybe. He knows where the tramps are in town."

"I admire Richard, *Süsse*. He has *caritas*. That is the main emotion of Jean Valjean from Victor Hugo's *Les Misérables*. It means something like your word *charity*. It means an active, outgoing love for others. Have you read *Les Misérables*?"

"You know I haven't."

"Both Richard and Slater have *caritas*. They try to make things better for people. Slater with his beautiful music and Richard with his giving ways and his word games. I don't think Richard is appreciated. I feel sorry for him."

"You feel sorry for everyone, if you ask me."

"No, that is you," Elisa said. "My mother thinks both you and your mother are underdog lovers. You stick up for tramps and miscreants."

"I don't stick up for miscreants. I don't even know what miscreants are."

"The difference between you and me," Elisa continued as we walked past the rose garden, "is you pity the underdogs and I feel contempt for those who make people into underdogs. How does someone get the notion they are better than another?"

"Who do you mean?"

"Girls like the Chi Pis. Anyone who looks down on others. Sometimes my own mother does. She often thinks she is superior to others."

"To my family?"

"I never said that, *Süsse*."

"It's strange, anyway, that she never speaks to us."

"Oh, of course she would speak to you if she saw you."

"She sees me," I said.

14

SLATER CARR

WHEN THE WARDEN'S daughter was not home, Carr could go there for away time. The warden said, "If my wife or Myra, the maid, appears, you are to ignore them."

When Myra went out to hang up clothes in the backyard, Slater would try to smile at her, touch his head in a little salute, almost manage a hello. The warden had told Slater she was on probation and could do housework off grounds until her freedom was granted.

Slater thought of his own mother, said to be crazy, sent to the Peachy Insane Asylum in her teens, pregnant, only to learn later a lot of girls like that weren't tetched at all; there just wasn't anyplace else to put them. When their babies were born, the POA took them in and raised them. That's how he wound up there.

Myra wouldn't look at him.

"She afraid of me?" he asked Warden Myrer once.

"Her freedom's coming up in another two years. She just doesn't want to get in trouble."

"I wouldn't hurt her."

"If she smiled at you, someone might say she was asking for it. She could even lose her away privileges."

"Some of us just don't ever get lucky, do we, boss?"

"Focus on now, Slater, not then."

First time the Warden didn't call him Mr. Carr.

15

THE FOURTH OF July, Richard showed up alone for the band concert and asked if he could sit with us.

"Where's Seth?"

"Over there," said Richard. I looked in the direction Richard pointed and saw Seth with J. J. Joy.

"What is he doing with her?"

"She's his date for the concert. Do you want to know something else?" He didn't wait for an answer. "Seth's fallen for her. It's been going on since January."

"I thought she couldn't date until she was seventeen."

"She was seventeen the first of July. Seth's been trying to butter up her father for months. Seth never cared about rescuing impounded cars last winter. He just wanted to save Mr. Joy's car. He thinks J. J.'s father hung the moon!"

"How could this happen right under our noses?" I said.

"They haven't been right under our noses," said Richard.

"They've been sneaking off together."

"I can't believe she'd sneak off with Seth," I said. "She hardly speaks to me. Just because she's the Cowpie president, she thinks she's queen of High East!"

"She's not so hotsy-totsy anymore," said Richard.

Cayutians were still in shock about the collapse of Joystep Shoes. It had been the town's leading industry.

"I think that J. J. Joy looks hotsy-totsy," said Elisa. "All the Cowpies do, which doesn't mean I like them. But I would like a gardenia for my hair too."

"It's not a real flower," Richard said.

"I would still like it."

J. J. Joy wore her dark-red hair pageboy style, a tight white sweater, and a flowered skirt. It was said she had ambitions to go to New York City one day and be a Powers model.

After a selection of band favorites, Slater Carr walked to the microphone with my father, who had worn his best summer suit, a white linen one, with a light-blue-and-white polka-dot tie.

My mother was off in Rochester, New York, at her semiannual physical examination to thwart any return of her old nemesis, pneumonia.

I always thought my father looked handsome enough to be in the movies. That was before Heinz Stadler came roaring up the street in his Duesenberg.

Now there was a new contender.

Slater Carr was not very tall. What was most noticeable about him was this angel face he had. It was like the faces of cherubs painted on the stained glass windows at Holy Family Church. He had light-green eyes, and straight white teeth when he smiled. But he was not a smiler—anyone could tell that. He had the expression of a small boy who had been sent to his room for something he did not do. He stood military straight on the bandstand, the slight breeze blowing a lock of his golden hair to his forehead.

His tan was too bronze for him to have gotten it in the prison yard. The cons took turns, there were so many of them. One never spent more than half an hour a day out there.

My father must have been giving Slater Carr a lot of away work. I knew he didn't get that color in our yard, because thanks to my mother, he didn't come to our yard anymore. My mother'd said, "Miss Germany gets too excited, and I am not going to be responsible for her making a fool of herself over one of our inmates."

"How fortunate we are to have Mr. Slater Carr with us," my father began. "How many have heard him play Taps evenings?"

There was wild applause, even from the band behind him.

Although Slater Carr got red, he didn't smile or take a bow.

"Like most fine musicians, Mr. Carr is not limited to one instrument." My father continued. "You know he can play the bugle, but right now he is going to treat us all to his talent with the trumpet." I couldn't believe the jovial sound to my father's voice. Even Richard gave me a puzzled look, his nose wrinkled with questioning: What's gotten into your old man?

"Watch out, music lovers!" my father bellowed. "Here's The Blues's answer to Louis Armstrong. I give you *Slater Carr*!"

More applause. My father must have told Slater Carr to smile when he introduced his number, because then he did, so quickly you had to have your eyes glued to his face to see it.

"I am going to play a song called 'Till Times Get Better,'" Slater Carr said.

"I never heard that song," I said.

Both Elisa and Richard stabbed my sides with their elbows. "Shhhhh!" they said.

16

WE HAD TO sit in our seats until the entire band marched off to the orange vans waiting to take them up Resurrection Hill. Richard was scratching himself, but I couldn't see any mosquitoes. I knew my father had sent some prisoners to the park earlier, to apply bug spray.

Now the prisoners went single file, holding their caps in their hands, heads bent, making no eye contact with the audience.

As they marched away, Elisa told me that she had waited all her life to hear someone play the trumpet like that.

"I could fall in love with him just for the reason of how he plays," she said. "But he is locked up for his whole life, so how can I feel the way I now feel?"

I shrugged. "You said yourself love is filled with pitfalls!"

Richard had fallen behind us, still scratching.

"It is so unbearably sad what happened to him because of love," said Elisa.

"Very, very sad," I said. I loved making things up for Elisa. She was like an actress, her eyes opening wide, her hands flying to her cheeks, cussing in German, in English saying something was unbearably sad or unbearably beautiful.

Richard had been tagging along silently. He finally spoke up. "What's the story on that Slater Carr?"

I said, "What's the story on you? You've been scratching your arms all night."

"I'm allergic to something," Richard said.

"Slater Carr committed a crime of passion," I told him.

"Another crime of passion?" Richard said suspiciously. "Who did he kill?"

"Jessica can't give away prison secrets," said Elisa, winking at me, "but my whole family is musicians, except for my father, so I know one thing about Slater. He is a genius."

"I know music too," said Richard. "I play the accordion."

"And you play the comb," I said, but Richard wasn't in the mood to kid around.

He said, "I know you know music, Elisa. I heard you

play the piano once when I went by a practice room at school."

"Thank you, Richard," said Elisa. "Someday, Jessica, I'll come to your house and play the piano for you."

"The Sontags have a piano," I said. Summer nights past, Gertie Sontag would play loud, trying to drown out my mother.

The pair had an affectionate rivalry over everything from their serenades to the elaborate hats they made for their grand appearances Easter Sundays at Holy Family.

"If we only did have a piano," said Elisa. "My mother misses so a piano. She does not sing now without one."

"What could have happened to the Sontags' baby grand?"

"They did not pay for all of it, so it was taken, right before we moved in."

"My mother didn't know that. . . . You know, your mother could play our piano. You can too."

"I do not think your mother likes me, Jessica. I do not think she is glad I'm your neighbor."

"Wrong!" I said. "My mother was afraid the Goldmans were going to buy the Sontag house. Then we would have had the first Jews in the neighborhood, right across the street from us."

There were not many Jews in our town. The nearest

synagogue was in Syracuse, twenty-eight miles away. The one thing our neighbors agreed on where Jews were concerned was that if they moved to a street, all the houses would automatically sell for less money.

"Does your mother want the neighborhood to be *Judenrein*?" Elisa asked me.

"I don't know what that means."

"It means 'Jew free.' Is that what your mother wants?"

"We don't own our house; the prison does," I said. "But the neighbors were all worried the Goldmans would move in where the Sontags are. Do you have Jew-free neighborhoods in Potsdam?"

"If *Dummkopf* Herr Hitler had his way, all would be, but the German people are not prejudiced as Americans are," said Elisa. "Many of my father's colleagues at the university are Jewish. In Germany we revere intellectuals."

"*Dummkopf* Herr Hitler!" Richard laughed. "That's good!"

I put my first finger up to my lips to make a mustache and cried, "*Dummkopf* Herr Hitler!" doing the goosestep walk I'd seen his soldiers do in newsreels.

"Shhhhh," said Elisa. "People look now at us."

"Let them look," I said, elbowing Richard, expecting him to agree with me. Since when did we care if people looked? But Richard wasn't himself. I figured he had poison ivy or something to make him so quiet except for the sound of him scratching himself everywhere.

Elisa said, "This has been a special evening."

"Because of you, Elisa," Richard managed to mumble. It was as hard for him to compliment anyone female as it was for a cat to laugh. Because of his braces, Richard was shy with all girls except me. His face was red. "I have to go, Elisa. We have to solve my problem too, or I will scratch myself bloody. See you!" He scurried along a path that led away from Elisa and me. No good-bye to me.

It was almost dark, and then there would be fireworks.

"What's Richard's big problem? Why is he itching so?"

Elisa said, "There's something I want to talk to you about, Jessica. I know you are a cheerleader for the unlucky ones in life, and that is what I admire about you. You will be glad to hear that Richard has captured Scruffy."

"The tramp's dog? Why didn't you tell me?"

"It was to be your surprise when the firecrackers go off. I told Richard to leave before, so you and I can decide something."

"Where is Scruffy?"

"He's at the Nolans', but he can't stay there. Richard is allergic."

"That's why he's scratching."

"Yes. . . . Jessica, can we give Scruffy to Wolfgang Schwitter? That mean tramp would never know the dog was on Lakeview Avenue. You can't even see the Schwitter house from the street. I've tried!"

"But would Wolfgang take him?"

"Remember last winter he spoke of his dachshund dying? Scruffy must have dachshund in him." Elisa laughed. "He's a little sausage! I name him Wurst!"

"Wurst Schwitter," I said, and the first rocket of the night zoomed above us.

17

SLATER CARR

HE'D FIND HIMSELF singing the same song over and over, about Georgia, about having Georgia on his mind. Nobody could have told him he'd ever be homesick for the place, but he was.

Inmates on The Hill didn't know the song was about the state of Georgia. They'd ask him, "What's she like, your Georgia?" He'd tell them, "She's beyond description; I don't have words to describe her."

The first time he ever heard "Georgia on My Mind," Purr played it for him and told him all about the man who wrote it, Hoagy Carmichael.

"He was your kind, Slater, a musician down to his bones," she said. "His mother used to play piano for silent movies, was where he got his love of music. She sent him off to the university in Indiana, and he got a law degree. So with his law degree he naturally set off to be a musician. He could have had a degree in you-name-it, wouldn't change his destination. You're like that too. Guess what else you share with Hoagy?"

"What else, ma'am?"

"How many people you going to meet in a lifetime called what you're called?"

"How many people had a midwife named Anne Slater deliver them? No, I never heard of another Slater."

"You ever hear of another Hoagy?"

Miss Nellie Purrington, called Purr by students at Peachy School, taught music, history, English, and geography. She could play the trombone, the trumpet, the cornet, and the saxophone. Slater had her all eleven grades. He'd stay after class to clean the erasers and empty the pencil sharpeners. He learned about all the composers from Hoagy Carmichael to Bix Beiderbecke to Lorenz Hart, and how to play the piano, the harmonica, the trumpet, and the bugle.

His favorite composer of all of them remained Hoagy Carmichael, and the song he liked best, of course, was called "Georgia on My Mind."

18

It was early Saturday night, warm the way July evenings are upstate New York.

Sometimes my father would call from the prison and announce that he was having dinner there. It was his habit to drop into the mess hall now and then unannounced, to show the inmates that he kept the cooks on their toes. They saw that whatever was good enough for them to eat was good enough for the warden too.

"I suppose Dad thinks he's some kind of hero because he does that," said Seth.

"He *is* a hero to eat that food," said my mother. "We're so overpopulated, it's hard to serve decent fare." Our mother always said "we" and "us" when she was talking about the prison. "This depression is as hard on us as it is on anyone."

Seth said, "They're not eating steak up there—you can bet on that."

The Myrers *were* eating steak. Mother had won two dollars in a bridge tournament and had planned to surprise Daddy that night. Then he'd called to say he would eat on The Hill. The superintendent of prisons was visiting.

Nights my father wasn't present for dinner, we ate in the dinette instead of the dining room. Nights he didn't come home in time to walk around the block with Mother, she would occasionally ask me if I wanted to walk with her.

I wasn't crazy about hearing everything that was wrong with me while we strolled along, from my posture to what Mother called my "fantasy" that Elisa Stadler was my friend. Seth would walk with her readily. She never found fault with Seth.

Olivia Myrer, animal lover supreme, had been told by Elisa and me, just before Seth arrived for dinner, that Wolfgang Schwitter had adopted the wire-haired brown dog, now called Wurst. Richard had taken him to Lakeview Avenue himself. My mother merely said, "All's well that ends well." She was too excited to have Seth home for dinner. She had gone on to fuss over the special Thousand Island dressing Seth liked on his salad, and where was his favorite yellow sweater he'd been missing for weeks? There was a white *M* on the right sleeve.

At the table Seth said, "We don't have it hard, Mom.

You want to know who has it hard because of this depression? J. J.'s father."

"Oh, well," said my mother, "I know people who worked for him, and that's another story."

"Why is that another story?"

"Those people don't have enough to eat," Mother said. "They don't have savings like the Joys do."

"He lost everything, Mother. His business. His name. They don't have savings either!"

"People like the Joys land on their feet, dear."

"The Joys may have to move to Iowa," Seth said.

"Oh, they won't have to move, honey. Something will come up. Something always does."

"He's really down in the dumps. He's drinking!"

"Drinking?" My mother's ears pricked up.

"You must never tell this."

"Of course not!"

"J. J. says he sneaks drinks. They keep a bottle of scotch in a cabinet in the dining room. J. J. sees him going in and out of there with his coffee mug. He spikes his coffee."

I knew my mother was in seventh heaven! Later that night she would be on the phone to one of her girl friends. Often her conversations began, "Wait till you hear this!"

"Hard times make everyone blue," said our mother.

"I'm not talking about feeling blue," said Seth. "I'm not talking about Dad's fretting over his precious prison, unaware there's a world going on outside The Hill! What's happening to the Joys is a monumental disaster! J. J. even worries Mr. Joy might kill himself!"

I couldn't help myself. I put down my fork and made gestures as though I were giving someone's phone number to the operator. I said, "Wait till you hear this. Horace Joy is getting pie-eyed nights because he's lost his shoe company. He goes into the dining room—"

"Jessica Osborne Myrer!" my mother exclaimed. "Just what are you doing?"

"Imitating a certain someone gossiping," I said, knowing it was one of those bad moves, the kind I had sometimes been compelled to make right before I met Elisa. I would get home and immediately be sent to my room for misbehaving in school: dropping Alka-Seltzer tablets in the inkwells, making the ink rise and spill across desks; letting the air out of teachers' tires; spreading gossip my mother told on the telephone.

"Mom would never tell something I told her in confidence," Seth said. "And Mom would never spread rumors about Mr. Joy!"

"We think the world of Horace Joy," Mother answered. She gave me the evil eye and said, "Go to your room. You're not having dessert."

Seth now viewed J. J.'s father the way he might a king who had lost his throne. Seth would remain his loyal

subject even after the basket under the guillotine contained Horace Joy's head.

"Just when I thought you were beginning to grow up,"
said my mother as I was leaving the table. "You're the
same old tomboy show-off. Someday tell me where on
earth Elisa Stadler got the idea the name Jessica suits you."

"You were the one who named me that."

"I didn't know how you were going to turn out," said
my mother, "or I never would have."

19

EARLIER, ELISA HAD come by on Gertie Sontag's bike and said she was going to Hollywood Hangout for ice cream for her father. Richard was with her. Lately he was with her every chance he got. Last week he had left a fake gardenia on the Sontag porch. Mother had seen him do it, and she had told me that no young man was going to buy a flower for me as long as I rode down streets on my bicycle no hands. "Boys do that sort of thing on bicycles, not girls. Not girls boys give flowers to."

Heinz and Sophie Stadler were sitting on the front porch swing across the street, holding hands. After I was sent to my room, I watched them from my bedroom window and wondered again about my own embarrassing family. Something was radically wrong with my parents. My mother was caring enough on the surface, but she seemed to pull back at any demonstration of affection—not that there was any coming from me. I knew she favored Seth, knew he was honey and darling and I was Jess—or Jessica Osborne Myrer when she was furious.

But my mother seemed not to want Daddy's touch either, despite their walking rituals and their grasshoppers. How could Daddy stand not being hugged or kissed? I couldn't remember a time they'd acted like lovers, except in old photographs around the house. They looked a lot younger in them, too.

At the other extreme were Elisa's parents. No wonder Elisa got out of the house when he was around. I'd seen that sort of thing only in the movies: long clinches, fingertip kissing, and staring into each other's eyes. Then he'd always light the two cigarettes and pass her one.

As I stared at them from my window, there was a knock on my door.

"Sweetie?" My father's whisper. "Ready for some dessert?"

I let him in, and Mugshot, the cat, slid through the door with him. My father had a slice of chocolate pie on a plate and a glass of milk.

"How did you sneak this up here?"

"Your mother is taking a walk with Seth. She told me you were being punished."

He sat down on my bed.

"What happened at dinner?" he asked.

"I was a *Dummkopf*." Then I told him all about it.

"You were asking for it, weren't you?"

"I guess."

"I thought since your friendship with Elisa, you haven't been teasing your mother. She can never take a joke, you know."

"You tease her too. You make fun of her when she makes those malapropisms."

"Oh, that's all in fun."

"Seth doesn't think so. He thinks you're belittling her."

"He's going through a stage, Jess. He doesn't like me right now. I went through it with my own father."

"And Mother's cold. I don't know why you like such a cold woman."

"I love her, Jessie."

I plugged my ears. My father pulled my hands down gently.

"You love her too," he said. "I thought you'd changed since you became friends with Elisa. You've grown up. But we don't lose our old ways overnight. I know that, honey. Old behavior is hard to shed," he said. "That's why we have so many recidivists up on The Hill."

"Are there more of them there than one-timers like Slater Carr?"

"There used to be. Nowadays life inside is easier than life outside, so some men do something purposely, to come back to us."

"I bet Slater Carr would never come back if he got out."

"He'll never get out," my father said emphatically. "And I think Mr. Carr is learning to make the best of it."

"Once I get out of here," I said, "I won't be back."

"You think of this house as a prison?"

"This town is. In my school they don't even read important books like *Les Misérables*."

"What's stopping you from checking it out of the library?"

"Because it's a hard book. I would never read it unless it was a school assignment."

"Oh, honey, you're just blue tonight because you had a fight with Mother."

"I'd like to see something of the world. I'm tired of being a hick! I may not finish high school."

"Okay. Will you write home?" A smile tipped his lips.

"It isn't funny, Daddy."

My father changed the subject. "Seth seems unhappy about a lot of things. Do you think so?"

"He's only unhappy about one thing. He's worried about J. J.'s father because he's broke and he's drinking."

"Oh, I don't think Seth need worry," said Daddy. "I'm

in Rotary with Horace. He's a levelheaded fellow. Shall I tell you a secret?"

"Okay."

"You're not to tell anyone. Not anyone! It could cost me my job."

"I promise I won't spill the beans."

"I have Mr. Carr helping Horace out. Mother told me Mrs. Stadler doesn't like prisoners working here, so Mr. Carr will do his away work at the Joys'."

"I wondered where the prisoners were."

"I'm not a hero. A lot of us are helping Horace. The Rotary saw that his car was paid up. I know that the Joys can't afford a gardener anymore, so Mr. Carr is doing his lawn, mowing it, pulling weeds and that sort of thing. Mother's sending Myra over one day a week as well."

"Does Seth know?"

"If he knows, he hasn't mentioned it to me. Your brother doesn't talk to me very much anymore."

"He doesn't talk to me, either. He does all his talking to Mr. Joy, I bet."

"Could be, sweetie."

When I finished the pie and milk, my father said he had one more surprise for me. He opened the bedroom door, reached down on the hall rug for something, and came back with a poster still rolled up.

"Baby Face Nelson?" I said.

"Nope."

"Pretty Boy Floyd?"

"Unt-uh." He shook his head.

Then he unrolled the sheet, and I saw:

MOST WANTED
SLATER
"GOLDILOCKS"
CARR

WANTED AS AN ACCOMPLICE
IN THE MURDER OF JEFF NAYBOR
IN WEEDSPORT, NEW YORK

REWARD!

I threw my arms around his neck. "Thank you!"

"You're welcome, sweetie pie."

"He looks younger than twenty. Look at that baby face!"

"I look at it every day, and I think what a waste it is to have him locked up. Here's a young man who never finished high school, never went on dates, never went on a picnic, owned a bike, a boat, a dog. No family anyone knows about."

"Who taught him how to play the bugle?"

"He's self-taught, I suspect."

"Doesn't he ever tell you about himself?"

"Very little. I don't encourage it. He has to live in the here and now."

"You never told me his nickname was Goldilocks."

"I don't call my inmates by their nicknames. I want them to think of themselves as men. Men who keep their nicknames into adulthood aren't taken seriously, in my opinion. Who would follow my orders up on The Hill if I still called myself Blocker?"

The poster made up for the fact I wasn't allowed to meet Elisa that night.

On the phone I told her I had a huge surprise for her. No, I would not tell her about it. Elisa had to see it.

At nine thirty sharp I went to the window. Most Cayutians had gotten used to his bugle by then. I had the feeling some, like me, stopped what they were doing and listened with the feeling of tears behind their eyes. When that happened to me, I was surprised. It had nothing to do with Slater Carr, but what was it making me sad?

Elisa said that when Slater played, she thought of

what her favorite American poet, Sara Teasdale, said about beauty.

> For beauty more than bitterness
> Makes the heart break.

I felt that I was on the verge of understanding poetry, on the verge of having more feelings than I'd ever had too.

But I was still only on the verge. I'd even tried reading T. S. Eliot ever since the librarian said Mrs. Stadler read him. At first I believed I had found a poet who could speak in plain, understandable language, but within a few lines I would find myself lost. I would stumble on

> Twit twit twit
> Jug jug jug jug jug
> So rudely forc'd . . .

and worse.

"Tell me something beautiful that could make your heart break," I asked Elisa.

"Richard. When he gave his coat to the tramp last winter. That was beautiful. It made me cry to know about it."

"Richard's not very beautiful with those rubber bands popping out of his mouth and hickies all over his face."

"It's what's inside him. He cares."

"*Caritas*. I remember."

"And it takes courage to care, I think. I don't have it. I talk about it, but what do I do? Maybe I will grow up to be like *Mutter*. Inside, a stone."

"My mother too."

"No. She is different with her tramps and her animal love. My mother loves only my father, me, and Omi, my grandmother. But we are part of her. It's when you care about something beyond you."

"What will become of us, Elisa?"

"I know. I will be at the top of the Eiffel Tower sometime in the future, waiting for you to overcome your fear of things at a slant. You have to get over it, you know. All of life is at a slant."

20

SLATER CARR

MISS PURRINGTON ALWAYS told Slater Carr she knew him like the back of her hand.

The trouble was that no part of Purr's anatomy could help her understand Slater Carr once Daisy Raleigh hit Peachy.

"Hit" would be the best way to put it, too, because she came roaring into town in a bright-red Pierce-Arrow, slamming smack into the Caribbean cabbage palm tree in front of Peachy School.

Sixteen years old, daughter of a judge from Auburn, New York, Daisy was driving from Savannah to Atlanta to meet her father. Judge Raleigh was there attending his sister's funeral.

Nellie Purrington had made the mistake of saying, "Help her, Slater. I think that young lady is off her rocker speeding that way."

For the one and only time in his life, Slater fell in love. She was wild and beautiful, and she could get him to do anything.

He would have followed Daisy anywhere, and he did—to Auburn, the Finger Lakes town in upstate New York where the Raleighs lived.

Two years from the day she leaned against him laughing, her long blond hair in her beautiful blue eyes, as Slater led her away from the smoking automobile, judge Raleigh had had it! It was not the first time she'd done something crazy, with someone she hardly knew, but the judge never put any blame on her. He got a court order forbidding Carr to come within ten miles of Auburn. Carr found a job pumping gas, seven miles away, living in a room above the service station.

Daisy Raleigh took the telephone during one of Slater's dozens of calls to the family home and told him when to meet her in front of the Naybor Pancake Shop. Her Pierce-Arrow would be out front, where he should get behind the wheel and wait for her. He would have to be on time and prepared to take off immediately, because she would be running from her father.

Actually, Daisy was running from Mr. Naybor. She had her father's pistol tucked into the waistline of her jeans and bills of all denominations crammed into a gym bag. There was the sound of gunfire and steps running toward Slater. Daisy dropped to the ground, which was where he last saw her, in a pool of her own blood.

She died there, with Mr. Jeff Naybor dead too, on the steps where Naybor had shot at Daisy.

Slater got in the Pierce-Arrow and escaped the law for one month, hiding five miles away at the Won't You Come Inn, washing dishes in the diner across the street.

One of the arresting officers had witnessed the crime, seen Slater race away, then made it his business to find him eventually and take him in.

"You never should have run, Goldilocks."

"Oh, sure, I'd get a break around here. I had to run!"

"It's over now, Goldilocks."

"Stop calling me that."

"That's my name for you. "

That was the first time anyone had ever called him by a nickname. He rode in the backseat of the patrol car thinking that the dead girl was as strange to him as the nickname. What had he ever really known about her?

Although he told the police he knew nothing about a plan to rob the pancake shop, no one believed him. He was an accomplice, no matter what he said to the contrary. Two people were dead, one the daughter of Judge A. G. Raleigh and the other the local sheriff's son, owner of the shop.

"You can pick 'em, Goldilocks," the arresting officer said. "You go before a judge with those two dead, you won't even be considered a nonkilling accomplice. They'll throw the book at you!"

21

IT WAS SUCH a scorching end of July, people were sleeping both in Hoopes Park and up by Cayuta Lake in Joyland Park. Some would just take blankets from their beds and go to the parks late at night, and others would make an event of it, packing coolers of cold drinks and sandwiches, their swimsuits, bathing caps, toy sailboats, and inner tubes.

We had to depend on fans. Standing, ceiling, window fans positioned throughout the house. When my mother was canning vegetables in the kitchen, she ordered a block of ice from the iceman. He put it in a pail near the fan, so it blew icy air at Mother and Myra from Elmira, who was always allowed to take a few jars back to her room at the reformatory.

Up on The Hill, honor inmates could sleep in the yard under the stars. That was a big treat for the dozen my father selected nightly. To keep fights from breaking out,

Daddy allowed the inmates to play chess and checkers in the common room after supper, although Taps at nine thirty remained the signal for lights out.

Elisa was teaching me to waltz. She would bring over her album of music from *Der Rosenkavalier* by Richard Strauss, and we would dance to the "Baron Ochs Waltz" up in my bedroom.

Soon school would begin. I would see in my mind's eye the two of us, going up the long circular walk with everyone by then used to the idea that we were fast friends. *"Guten Tag,"* I'd say when anyone said good morning, or perhaps just *Tag*, as Elisa sometimes said. *Tag, Süsse.*

Special times Elisa would treat me, after school, to an ice-cream soda I had invented: a strawberry soda with pistachio ice cream. We would share a booth in Hollywood Hangout. Elisa had a bigger allowance than I did, and she declared that in return for buying me the soda, I must tell her any tale I could think of about the Chi Pis, who crowded into booths at Hollywood Hangout and all wore green socks on Thursdays.

I would tell Elisa the Cowpies were made to lie in closed coffins for hours as part of their initiation and, blindfolded, made to kneel by toilet bowls and fish out bananas that felt like turds, then eat them.

"Lieber Gott! Who told you?" Elisa would ask, eyes alert,

covering her mouth with her hand as though those around us could read lips.

"I can never tell my source." Some stories about the Cowpies I made up, and some I put together from rumors Seth had heard about frat boys' initiations at Cornell University. Seth, true son of Olivia Myrer, liked intrigue and scandal too.

Gone were the days when I would sit in Seth's room hanging on every word from his mouth. I began to think of those days as part of my childhood, silly really, and gone forever. Elisa had come into my life like some new color never before seen.

Daddy took Mother for an extra-long walk when it cooled just a trifle, despite the fact all weather reports promised the heat would return with a vengeance. They went all the way to downtown Cayuta and bought peanut sundaes at Hollywood Hangout.

"Even if he is not intimate with her, he seems to love her," said Elisa. "Last night he took her downtown for ice cream, *ja*?"

"He always takes her for walks! Big deal!"

"Why do you want to believe they do not have relations?"

"Because she's an icicle."

"Maybe not to him."

Elisa had put aside an English-language edition of Victor Hugo's *Les Misérables*. She was allowed an "open choice" veering from the summer reading list for tenth graders at East High. I was reading a new writer, Thomas Wolfe, copying lines into my diary like: "Which of us is not forever a stranger and alone?"

We were lollygagging about on the front porch swing, painting our toenails and drinking raspberry Kool-Aid. *Lollygag* was one of my father's favorite words. It meant "hang around and do nothing." My father had grown up down south, and southern expressions would slip into his speech now and then. He would say Mother was "strutting Miss Lucy," evenings she got all dolled up to go to dinner with him. He would say, "If you knock the nose, the eye will hurt," meaning if you hurt anyone in a family, the whole family felt it. Sometimes in the shower he would sing "Alabama Bound." He would clown around: "I'm Alabamy bound. . . ."

Across the street, Elisa's parents were getting into their black Duesenberg.

"Where are they off to?" I asked Elisa.

"My mother's driving him to the university."

"He's like my father, " I said. "He never gets time off." I was admiring the fit of Heinz Stadler's white pants. He was tall with long legs, and his trousers with their white belt gave his body a slender, sexy look. My father and brother never wore tight pants.

"He is not like your father. He is home every chance he gets. Family is everything to my father. You know what? Grandmother will live with us when she is finally here. That is the way my father is. He is devoted to family. And she is Mother's mother, not even his own."

"When is she coming here?"

"Soon. She is trying to sell her house. She is very old, and my father says we cannot miss the opportunity to be with her in her end years."

I had nothing to say to that. My mother's parents had both died of alcoholism at early ages. My father's lived in the south, still regretting the fact their only son lived up north and had not carried on the family tradition and become a dentist. Every two or three years the Alabama Myrers traveled to upstate New York for an awkward Christmas or Easter dinner with us. Arguments would break out and then be quickly stopped with my mother's reminders it was a holiday and we hardly ever saw one another.

My grandmother would say things like "When we do see one another, there's always a penitentiary right outside the windows! And it takes hours and hours to get here!" . . . We never went down south to see them. Daddy would not leave The Hill that long.

Elisa said, "I have a surprise for you."

"What?"

"We have been invited to the Schwitters'."

"We have?" I was amazed. "I don't even know them. Did you get me invited?"

"I'm sorry, Jessica. I put it a wrong way. Tonight I have to go there with my parents. The Schwitters are having a party."

"And you were invited?"

"My father has been talking to Herr Schwitter about Omi, my grandmother. Herr Schwitter has relatives in Germany too."

"Will you tell me everything that happens there? I've always been curious about the Schwitters' parties."

"Yes. Of course I'll tell you."

"Every detail, the way I tell you things. What I like to know is what is said, what is strange, and what suspicions you might have."

"Suspicions?"

"Secrets, undertones, the way I told you about Slater Carr. Remember? The fire, the naked man, that kind of thing."

"I don't think that kind of thing will be there, Jessica."

"Just keep your eyes and ears open for anything juicy!"

"I will try. Do you want to see the new dress I bought for the occasion?"

"Not right now."

I didn't feel like waiting for Elisa to go across the street, change her clothes, return in a dress, then go back again.

I wore white shorts and a shirt of Seth's I'd cut the sleeves out of. I wore my old white sneakers I was always thinking of cleaning but never did. Still, I was hands down more presentable since Elisa had entered my life. I actually believed I was even slightly sophisticated and when I was exasperated I would say *Bitte!* as Elisa did: Please! At other times, when I wanted something, I would say *Bitte?* sweetly.

"Please come with me while I make sure my dress fits."

"You mean go over to your house with you?"

"Yes, unless you would rather wait here."

I almost never felt my heart react to anything, but now I could feel it moving under my shirt.

"I'll tell my mother where I'll be," I said.

Elisa screwed the top of the nail polish on tightly and stood up. "If you hate my new dress, do not say so. Please?"

"It'll probably be just fine, for a dress."

"I like to dress up," said Elisa.

"I don't hate it myself," I said. "It's just that there's not much reason to dress up around here." My voice had a strange hoarse tone to it as I called out, "Mother? I'm going across the street to Elisa's."

Silence.

"Faculties back in my homeland have parties regularly,

and the wives and children of professors are invited. I have always dressed up, all my life, and I miss that here," said Elisa.

Mother's voice from inside the house. "You're going where?"

"Across the street," I said, my heart beating wildly.

22

THERE WAS NOTHING in particular to see. The Sontags' same old shabby davenport and claw-leg chairs with antimacassars on the armrests, an oriental rug so worn the design didn't show, a round table (where the piano used to be) covered with a skirt, a vase of daisies resting on top.

There were photographs in frames beside the vase.

I picked up one showing a younger Elisa sitting in a swing, a smiling woman behind her, ready to give her a push.

On the woman's sweater was the gold dachshund pin that Elisa always wore, the same one Wolfgang Schwitter had tried to buy.

"That is Almighty Ida," said Elisa. "My grandmother." She grinned at me. "Oh, how she will hate living in America!"

"Has she ever been here?"

"No. She does not think Americans are interested in culture. Already she is putting down her feet." Elisa laughed. "*Sie spielt die beleidigte Leberwurst!*" She was starting upstairs. "That means 'She's playing the prima donna.'"

I said, "You don't put down your feet. You put your foot down."

"*Grossmutter*'s foot is definitely down when it comes to the United States of America! It is not just the dangers here, but also the looks of things. Potsdam is so beautiful, *Süsse!*"

Elisa said that her grandmother was once a famous opera star, but now she owned an antiques shop in a small town near Potsdam. "She would faint—how do you say it?—she would keel over if she saw this." She held up the poster of Slater I had given her.

She said she would never be allowed to hang it in her room. She wished I would keep it for her. She had pasted a handwritten poem on it, copied from a book of Constantine P. Cavafy's poems. Cavafy was a favorite of her parents'. This poem her father had once sent her when she was having a hard time at a new school.

"When you hang Slater's poster in your room, Jessica, you will have these words for him, even though he'll never read them. I believe they will carry in the air to his soul and soothe him."

AS MUCH AS YOU CAN

Even if you cannot shape the life you want,
try this, at least
as much as you can; don't demean it
in too much contact with the world,
in too many movements and too much talk.

Don't demean it by taking it,
spinning it about and exposing it
to the everyday foolishness
of relationships, of alliances,
til it becomes a tiresome, alien life.

CONSTANTINE P. CAVAFY (1913)

"Slater Carr won't have to worry much about coming into too much contact with the world," I said.

"Will you take Dillinger's poster down and put this one in its place?"

"I'll have both up. Now that John is loose, he might need something in the air to soothe his soul."

"I think he has a different kind of soul," said Elisa. "I don't think he is as deserving of anything in the air to soothe him."

How easily we talked of Slater and John, almost as

though they were members of our families or close in some other, undefined way. While Elisa had made it plain she did not admire Dillinger, we both would chatter away about Slater Carr, imagining his life before The Hill. I think we talked about him more than we cared about him. I think he was someone we could love safely together, no rivalry, no qualms about what he was. He was being punished for that. Unlike Dillinger, he was not the sort of habitual convict whose mind was always contemplating escape.

Dietrich was sleeping on a pillow. Elisa picked her up and hugged her as she talked. "*Grossmutter*—I call her Omi—she thinks America is filled with Dillingers," said Elisa. "She and my *Mutter* prefer to be at home. Not my father. He loves everything about America. He began speaking English to me when I was a little child."

"What if she refuses to come here?"

"She will come because of my mother. Mother is going there in a few months to bring her back here. My father will join the faculty at Cornell University next year. Poor Omi is afraid to live here. She is like my mother, who feels safe only in Germany."

"Who does your mother think would hurt her?"

"First, the prisoners up on The Hill. Then your cowboys. Your Indians. Your gangsters. That Crazy Carl."

"Carl wouldn't hurt anyone. He's just mentally retarded."

"What about the prisoners? Even I sometimes am afraid the prisoners will break out!"

"I don't believe you."

"It's the truth, though, Jessica. You don't believe me and that's why I can confess it to you. Then I don't feel naïve because you don't believe me anyway," Elisa said. "My mother feels safe only in the library and at church."

"All the town nuts hang out in the library."

"Don't ever tell her that."

"I'll try to keep that in mind the next time your mother and I have a conversation."

"Now you become sarcastic." Elisa put Dietrich back on the pillow and changed the subject. "My kitty is attached to my odor, I believe. She wants to be only near me or something of mine," she said. "I am flattered!"

Dietrich fled as I flopped spread-eagle on the bed.

"Do you think I'll ever go anywhere, Elisa?"

"You mean to Europe?"

"Anywhere! Europe, Africa, the Orient."

"Do you want to travel so badly?"

"You did that to me, Elisa. I want too much contact with the world! I want to be like you. Speak many languages. Like you."

"I want to be like you."

"Oh, what is there about me to envy?"

"You are a storyteller. You are sensational, unbearably sensational! And you are a great reader of the modern novel. You find out about the prisoners and the Chi Pis, and you know juicy secrets."

"What I know any hick with ears knows. I want to be someone who can tell about the elevator going up at a slant in the Eiffel Tower. I don't think I'll get farther away than California my whole life, if I even get there."

"I like America best if I can't be in Germany. Do you know that? I like the popular music. I like lollygagging around with you. I wish you were going to the Schwitters' too."

"Are you excited?"

"*Mutti* is. I guess I am too. That's why my father is going to Cornell. He does not have to work this week. His dinner jacket is there. On the invitation it reads black tie."

"Do you have to wear an evening gown?"

"A long dress. Want me to show you now?"

"Yes! Let's see it!"

"I will tell you everything that happens at the Schwitters'! You'll think you've been there. You know, I like describing things. I may become a travel writer someday."

"I wouldn't mind being a travel writer either. Then I'd see something of the world."

Elisa got up and walked to her closet. "We are soul mates."

"Yes, we are," I said.

"Through thin and thick."

"Through thin and thick," I agreed.

Just as Elisa was pulling her new dress over her shoulders, a voice called from downstairs.

"Girls? Where are you? Jess? Elisa?"

"That's not my mother?" I said, knowing it was.

23

MY MOTHER, RED-FACED, sitting in one of the Sontags' stuffed chairs, carpet slippers off, had just finished complaining that her corns and bunions hurt her when Sophie Stadler walked through the door.

"You have unexpected visitors," my mother said brightly, though I knew Mrs. Stadler was the last person she had expected or wanted to see.

White dress, white picture hat, white high heels, Sophie Stadler lighted a cigarette and shook her head with disbelief at whom she saw sitting there. She slipped the cigarette into a long silver holder, giving Mother a perfunctory nod, saying hello in such a quiet voice she might as well not have said it. She inhaled, exhaled, and sighed loudly.

Did my mother's feet stink or was I imagining it?

"I was just showing Jessica my dress, *Mutti*," Elisa said. "I thought you took *Vater* to Cornell."

"It is sweltering, and the traffic is captured by people who drive to the lake. Your *Vater* went on, and I walk back from town." Her English was not anywhere near as good as her daughter's.

I said, "My mother came over to get me, so we were showing her Elisa's dress too."

"I didn't come to get you," said Mother. "I came to tell you something I happened to hear on the radio."

"What?" I asked.

"Never mind now. Now is not the time. I will tell it to you later."

Mrs. Stadler's displeasure at finding us in her living room was very apparent. She frowned, and her nostrils flared when she spoke. Instead of speaking to my mother, she spoke to me.

"You must be my daughter's Jessica." She blew out yet another puff of smoke.

"Yes," I said. "And you are Mrs. Stadler. I've seen you in church."

"When you go to church," said Mrs. Stadler coolly.

"And I've seen you in the library too," I said.

"You don't see my daughter in church because she's not a good Catholic. I'm the good Catholic," said my mother. She was in one of her "housework" housecoats, a cotton rag splashed with an odd floral design and tomato and beet stains, left from last week's canning. "I'm the one you see in church!"

I knew that my mother had seen Heinz and Sophie Stadler drive away and had crossed the street believing only Elisa and I would be in the Sontag house. She never would have appeared before Elisa's mother wearing a housecoat of any kind, much less the soiled one she had on. Maybe she had heard something important over the radio, and maybe she just wanted to see what the Stadlers had done with Gertie Sontag's house. Face-to-face with her nemesis, she was determined not to be forced out of there by a renter who fancied she was better than her neighbors.

My mother was fond of saying that she never saw Sophie Stadler with anyone but her husband or Elisa and that she bet her life Mrs. Stadler had no friends. That was often followed with the fact that at her own last birthday, Olivia Myrer had received fifteen birthday cards from dear friends. She never added that all came from the wives of guards on The Hill.

I knew my mother well enough to know that secretly she would give anything to have Mrs. Stadler's approval.

"I will go up and change, then meet you at your house," Elisa told me.

She wore white satin slippers, a simple white off-the-shoulder ankle-length silk dress, with a string of pearls around her neck.

"Yes, take off the dress immediately. It is for the party only," said Mrs. Stadler, avoiding any eye contact with the short redheaded woman who was trying secretly to slide her tortured feet back into her slippers.

I said, "Guess what, Mother! The Stadlers are going to the Schwitters' tonight for a party!" I knew deep down it was the wrong thing to say. What could my mother reply to that?

"Do you tell all our business?" Mrs. Stadler addressed the question to Elisa.

"Is it such a secret, *Mutter*?"

My mother slowly got her small body up out of the large cushioned chair. "The Schwitters and their fancy parties are old news to me."

Mrs. Stadler put her initialed platinum lighter and a pack of her French cigarettes on the round table near where my mother was standing.

"I knew it would not be an American cigarette," said my mother. "The smell is different. I gave up smoking when we moved here. I came down with pneumonia. It nearly killed me."

"Come on now, Mother," I said, for it was so obvious that Elisa's mother did not want us there. "We must go, Mother!"

Elisa's mother was a corner-of-the-mouth smoker. The Gauloise drooped from her lips, smoke curling up into the room. This started my mother coughing. Almost anything could, ever since her pneumonia.

"We've had our share of invitations up to the Schwitters'," she finally managed to continue. (Stop her, God! I prayed.) We had no more than a nodding acquaintance with the Schwitters. Reinhardt Schwitter was the only musician whose music my father seemed not to admire. He called him a "longhair highbrow."

"Speaking of my pneumonia," Mother continued, although Mrs. Stadler was looking everywhere but at her, "I took sick with it the very night of one of Reinhold Schwitter's fancy dances in their ballroom."

"Reinhardt, not Reinhold," I said softly.

My mother went on, "I couldn't go because I was ambulatory."

"Ambulatory?" Elisa asked.

"Waiting for the ambulance," said my mother.

Elisa covered her mouth to hide a smile. "Then I am mistaken. I thought *ambulatory* meant 'able to walk.'"

"We have to go, Mother. Now!" I said.

"Well, it has been an honor to meet you, Mrs. Stadler," said my mother, bowing, shuffling forward in her slippers, hand extended. Then, when it was ignored, it was plunged into the pocket of her housecoat. She rocked on her heels. "We Myrers may not be as ritzy as the Schwitters, but my husband's father, Dr. Seth Merchant

Myrer, was a dentist of some renown in Montgomery, Alabama."

"I have a headache," said Mrs. Stadler. "I must lie down."

My mother said, "We'll talk another time. I would hope we could talk about many of the interesting facets of life in Cayuta. Oh, we aren't Europe, not by any means, we aren't the Taj Mahal or the London Bridge, but we have very lovely parks, a lovely lake, and country clubs. Two country clubs. There is the one for people of the Jewish persuasion, and there is the one for Christians. We Myrers are not joiners, though. We prefer—"

"Please. I am not well." Mrs. Stadler headed for the stairs.

"Mother? Come with me now," I said, praying that whatever my mother was going to say the Myrers preferred would not get said. What could it be that the Myrers preferred, snooping through venetian blinds at people with lives?

"Hold your horses, Jess," said my mother. "I'm coming."

"She's coming, Jessica." Elisa smiled. "See, she's ambulatory."

"Lay off her," I said under my breath. I remembered what my father sometimes said: If you knock the nose, the eye will hurt.

The sound of a door slamming upstairs shook the house.

My mother said to Elisa, "I hope nothing is wrong with your mother. Or did the wind do that?"

"I'm sorry," Elisa whispered to me. "I should not have said that about ambulatory."

I could feel my face in flames. "Never mind!"

"You're right to be angry, *Süsse*," Elisa whispered. "I like that you stick up for your mother."

But my mother never missed anything. "Oh, in a pig's eye," she said. "She never sticks up for me."

"She just did," said Elisa.

Now I had Mother by the arm, pulling her along. I said over my shoulder, "I'll get the poster later, Elisa."

24

Dear Slater,

Hello after a long time. I have gotten over my mad finally. I should have known of all my boys I could not have stayed mad at you. But maybe it was myself I was really mad at anyway, because I sit here hating to think I had a part in your crime.

I never should have asked you to help that hoyden from up north. Now is your chance to get out the dictionary and learn a new word if you don't know what a hoyden is. You were so proud of the headway we made putting The Georgia Peaches together before that day she ruined our tree out front. I could not believe you ran away from the band. I have to face the fact I could not have held you here. You had too much talent, and you are the type those kinds of girls fall for with your good looks.

I believe what you wrote about not knowing that girl had a gun. I know you, Slater, and you are no killer.

I am writing to get this off my chest because my heart is now going off on its own track when it feels like it and the doctors don't like it. I don't like it either. I was planning to save money and come north just so's I could see your smile one more time, put my hand in yours, and say I would give anything to take you back home with me.

And now I have said it.

Yours very truly and with love,

Nellie Purrington

25

THE NEW YORK TIMES

NEW YORK, MONDAY, JULY 23, 1934   TWO CENTS.

DILLINGER SLAIN IN CHICAGO; SHOT DEAD BY FEDERAL MEN IN FRONT OF MOVIE THEATER

◆ ◆ ◆

REACHED FOR HIS GUN

◆ ◆ ◆

OUTLAW'S MOVE MET BY FOUR SHOTS, ALL FINDING THEIR MARK

◆ ◆ ◆

HAD LIFTED HIS FACE; DESPERADO HAD ALSO TREATED FINGERTIPS WITH ACID

26

Good evening, Mr. and Mrs. America, from border to border and coast to coast and all the ships at sea. Let's go to press.

The 11,520-ton passenger liner Morro Castle *caught fire during a voyage between Cuba and New York and burned to a gutted shell. One hundred thirty-three persons, mostly passengers, were either drowned or burned to death.*

Two months had gone by since the party at the Schwitters'. What little Elisa told me about that night had to do with Wolfgang, which was why we were listening to Walter Winchell on a Sunday night in September. Elisa told me Wolfgang Schwitter said "everyone" listened to Winchell on Sunday evenings. Wolfgang was going to be a big theatrical producer one day. He was already in New York City working on a real Broadway musical called

Anything Goes. At the Schwitters' party, with Wurst wearing a new diamond collar and sitting beside Wolfgang on the piano bench, Wolfgang had sung a new song to Elisa. He had looked right at her the whole time. Because of the excitement he'd made her feel, she couldn't remember many of the words, just "your face in every flower, your eyes in stars above."

"Do we have to hear Winchell?" I complained.

"I thought you cared about Hollywood stars."

"There weren't any Hollywood stars on that ship. Walter Winchell would have mentioned it if there were."

"How do you know, Jessica? You never listen to him."

"I just know," I said. "He's a gossip columnist. My mother listens to him, and she reads him in *The Syracuse Post-Standard*."

"Turn it off if you can't stand it," Elisa said.

"You turn it off. It was your idea."

"It's your radio, Jessica."

"Leave it on. I don't care. . . . I hate geometry."

What I hated was hearing about Wolfgang all the time.

Because the September weather was like July, we were sitting on my front porch with the living room window open so we could hear the Stromberg-Carlson radio inside.

School had started. I was working on my geometry homework. Elisa was reading *Magnificent Obsession* by Lloyd C. Douglas, a book she said she had chosen from the bestseller list solely because of the title. She said she couldn't concentrate on anything. She kept remembering a conversation with Wolfgang, the night of the Schwitter party. She claimed he called her Phyllis as a joke, and I shot back I bet it wasn't a joke at all. She insisted it was. She said that whole evening had changed her.

"Because of him?" I said.

"You don't know what he was like with me."

"I don't know because you don't tell me."

"It's hard to describe it. It's a feeling more than anything else."

"Well, I can describe feelings. Why can't you?"

"I can't."

"What happened to 'I'll tell you everything that happens; you'll think you were there'? You haven't told me anything about that party except about him."

"I told you no one there mentioned Dillinger's death."

"No one there *would.*"

"That's what made your mother cross the street that day. She said she'd heard something on the radio. Remember?"

I didn't want to remember my mother's confronting Mrs. Stadler that afternoon at the Sontags'. I sank into a long silence.

Elisa finally said, "Jessica?"

"What?"

"Tell me something *honestly*, okay?"

"Okay," I said, wondering if she'd suddenly figured out I sometimes made up stories to tell her.

"If Wolfgang hadn't gone back to New York City, do you think he'd ask me out? Maybe not for a real date. Not yet. Maybe just for a ride in his car, top down, under the stars."

I groaned. "What do you mean, maybe not for a real date, *not yet*? Do you think Wolfgang Schwitter is going to date you?"

"He could," Elisa said. "You should have seen him sing that song to me the night of the party. Oh, Jessica, now I remember the name of that song. It's called 'The Very Thought of You.'"

"The very thought of Walter Winchell is making me nuts!" I said. I stormed into the house and snapped off the radio.

"Why are you angry?" Elisa asked when I went back to the porch.

"Who's angry?"

"Listen to your tone of voice."

"I don't listen to myself. I'm not like some people all caught up in themselves."

"Are you upset because of John's death?"

I had to think for a second who John was. Then I realized it was Dillinger.

"That was ages ago!" I said.

"It was the same time my family and I went to the Schwitters'."

"I don't care about Dillinger," I said. "I made a lot of that up."

"You did?"

"When Seth was collecting posters with me, I pretended to get all excited over Dillinger to please Seth. Then I guess I believed myself."

"I'm glad you told me that, *Süsse.* I began believing myself too about Slater Carr."

She said she had no deep feelings toward Slater Carr. She loved hearing him play. She loved his looks, and also she loved the things I had told her about him. But he was part of her make-believe, as movie stars were, and others she would never meet. She said she'd exaggerated all that to keep up with my interest in gangsters and inmates on The Hill. She added that she really did like knowing things I told her: how a man had killed his wife using only rhubarb leaves; how Bonnie and Clyde had nicked their wrists with a safety pin and then carved into their arms "Blood of my blood; heart of my heart."

"My mother thinks I'm in love with Slater. Let her think it!" Elisa said.

"I suppose *I* get the blame for it."

Elisa laughed. "You get the blame for everything. But no

matter what my mother says about you having a morbid interest in violence, I keep right on sticking up for you. I always will!"

I said, "You make it sound like you were sticking up for Hitler."

"That is Omi who sticks up for Hitler. Omi thinks he is going to save Germany."

"From what?"

"We have a depression too, you know. Over here you think the only depression in the world is yours."

From across the street came the bloodcurdling sound cats make moments before an out-and-out attack.

"Your turn," I said.

"I went last time."

"They were here last time. They're over at your house now."

Yyyyyyeeeeeeeeeeeeeooooooooooow.

Elisa jumped up from the hammock and ran down the front steps.

"It's Mugshot doing it," she shouted over her shoulder.

"Dietrich starts it!" I said, tossing my textbook onto the wicker table before running after Elisa.

As we reached the other side of the street, Mugshot fled past us with his hair on end, his tail swishing.

"Is that any way to treat a neighbor?" I called after him.

Elisa had Dietrich gathered in her arms, kissing her brow.

"She's purring. She's all right," she said.

It was then that Sophie Stadler appeared in the doorway of their house. No hello for me, of course, much less a glance in my direction.

She said, "Elisa! Telephone!"

"Tell Richard I'll call him later."

"Elisa, come to the telephone now. It is not Richard."

Elisa and I gave each other looks and shrugs.

"Who could that be?" I said.

"I have no idea," Elisa answered.

"Hurry, Elisa!" her mother said. "It is not a local call!"

I went back across the street, remembering Elisa telling me the family was bringing her grandmother from Potsdam to live with them. But before that an aunt was visiting in October; she was the twin sister of Mrs. Stadler.

I wondered if she would be the same cold fish.

27

Dear Slater,

In case I should not be around much longer, I want you to know I have left my sheet music and records to you. I have left money with my sister, Susan Purrington, for the postage.

Now I would send this on to you right now except for the fact I am still teaching and guess what! The Georgia Peaches are still playing, and we have two trombones!

We may never match The Jenkins Orphanage Band, but we can be proud of our boys, and I think of you every time they play "Till Times Get Better."

I remember how you loved Jabbo Smith, who, like you, has an unusual first name, which is Cladys. I have asked folks around here if anyone knows what became of him, but no one knows.

This is not the way I ever thought either of us would

wind up, you behind bars and me watching my ticker carefully.

God bless you, Slater. I enjoyed the card you sent and was surprised the prison looks so big compared to ours outside Atlanta.

XXX Nellie Purrington

28

THE HALLOWEEN PARADE would begin on Genesee Street at three P.M. For the first time in its history my dad had convinced the mayor to include the prison band. The Blues would wear their usual blue uniforms, but they would also be allowed to wear skeleton masks.

While The Blues practiced up on The Hill, my father was home for lunch. He was all excited about installing a new pressing machine in the prison laundry.

"The guards think this time I'm going too far," he told my mother and me. Seth was eating at school with J. J. Joy. Elisa was across the street lunching with her aunt, visiting from Potsdam.

"Arthur, I think you're going too far too," said my mother. "Why do their sort need their pants pressed?"

"Honey, there's not enough work for everyone. You know that. This will put quite a few inmates to work." Then Daddy said to me, "Don't forget the parade starts promptly at three. Slater will have a marching solo to kick things off."

My father'd stopped calling him Mr. Carr. Now he was Slater, the name Elisa and I called him. Our doing it was one thing, but Warden Arthur Myrer's doing it was a first. Sometimes he would pick Slater up himself wherever Slater was working instead of sending the prison van to get him. They would sit on some green, manicured lawn in the late afternoon smoking and talking. Seth had seen them and laughed to Mom that the prisoner was our father's pet.

While we ate macaroni and cheese with bacon crumbled up into it, I began another of my quizzes. I was just curious about Daddy and the prisoner. I'd never seen my father show such favoritism before.

"What do you talk about with Slater Carr?" I asked.

"What we say isn't very important. Small talk, that's all."

"But what do you say?"

"Oh, he's a tease sometimes. He says things like 'Copper Tom just winked at me, boss.'"

Copper Tom stood on top of the prison, a man-size copper guard dressed in the uniform of a continental sol- dier. No one inside the prison could see his face. Although his expression was stern, town legend had it that if Tom winked at you, you were doomed.

Very few prisoners ever saw Copper Tom's face unless

they worked outside the prison, but they all knew the legend of Tom's wink. Arthur Myrer and Slater Carr could see him from most places where they rested.

"He calls you boss? Not Warden?" I said.

Daddy shrugged and continued, "I asked him, 'Do you consider yourself doomed now, Slater?'"

"What did he say?"

"Well, he said he used to feel doomed, but he didn't feel that way at all anymore."

"Why doesn't he now?" I asked.

"I think there's a point when a Hill man becomes resigned, even satisfied. They forget about getting back outside, particularly lifers like Slater. They make the best of what they have. I try to help them do it. That's why I'll get their pants pressed"—a pointed look at my mother. "It's little enough to do for someone. The man has no family. He has no friends."

"Oh, and so you're his family," my mother said.

"Not his family, but his friend, yes. I'm not a friend of many of them, but I am of this boy. He's changed things for me and for The Blues, and for others too, in my opinion."

"For this whole town every night at nine thirty," I said. "And Elisa used to be afraid of the prison and the prisoners, but she's not anymore."

"I think he got your mind off Dillinger, too," my mother said to me. "I notice Dillinger isn't up on your wall. Just the

Bugle Boy, with that poem pasted to him."

"Dillinger's dead, Mother!" I reminded her. "Elisa put the poem there."

"You two ought to get yourselves some real boyfriends," said my mother, "and stop getting crushes on jailbirds."

That made me think of the change in Elisa. She had suddenly stopped talking about Wolfgang. Whatever that was about (out of sight, out of mind?), I was glad. Now if I could just get my father to stop talking about Slater! What had I started?

"You know, that boy has a beautiful voice too," he went on. "You should hear him sing. He knows songs I bet you never heard of before, very haunting ones. Love songs. 'Her Smoke and Smile,' 'Her Style,' and that other one, 'A Thirsty Woman Drank My Tears.'"

"You're right. I've never heard of such songs," said my mother.

"I think maybe they're Negro songs, blues, the kind I'd hear back home," said my father. "The boy grew up in Georgia. He sings them sometimes when we're heading home with this red, round sun leaving the sky. I get to wondering if I felt that way when I was young and just falling in love with you, Mother. Or is it the kind of sentiment invented by men who were never successful with love?"

My mother said, "Ask our new neighbors across the street. Every time he's home, you see Heinz Pickle and his wife mooning around on the Sontag porch. But European males are different, if you ask me. Germans, in particular, are different. Sentimental, crying in their beer oom-pah-pah types."

"I think we felt that way once, sweetheart."

"Oh, well, what if we did." It was not a question.

"I wish we were going to the parade, all of us," he said, "but I tag along on Slater's away performances too often. I heard him at the Fourth of July celebration, the Kiwanis Club luncheon, and the Four-H Hog Contest. He's playing two solos on the grandstand this afternoon."

My mother said, "I won't miss hearing him, and I won't miss that parade. It's for kids anyway, or people with little kids. I'm looking forward to dinner at Krebs."

"Me too, honey."

My father had promised to take her to an early dinner at their favorite place by the lake in nearby Skaneateles, New York. It was a sunny day, a fine day to drive over there. Of all the Finger Lakes, Skaneateles was my parents' favorite. They had spent much of their courtship sailing on that lake in a Comet from the boatyard my grandfather had managed. Those were their halcyon days. He often said so. That's how I learned the word. When I looked up *halcyon*, I was surprised to see "synonyms: peaceful, happy, ideal."

"Why are you surprised?" my dad had asked.

"I can't picture you two as lovebirds."

"We're not birds," he had answered. "But we are lovers."

"Stay safe," Mother called after Daddy when he headed back up to The Hill. That was as close as she came to showing him any affection. He blew a kiss at her and at me as he went out the door.

Mother said, "I don't know who deserted who: Did Daddy desert Seth or did Seth desert Daddy?"

"It doesn't matter," I said. "Seth has J. J. the Jerk now, and Daddy has Goldilocks."

"I think Daddy is happier since that boy came here. And The Blues are going to beat that New Orleans band this year, for sure!"

"We'll win the Black Baaa," I said. "At last!"

"Still, the rift between Daddy and Seth is getting deeper, Jess. I thought Seth having the Joy girl would make him softer, but now I think he even values Horace Joy over Daddy."

"That's one way Slater isn't a good thing," I said. "Seth resents him."

"Oh, Seth isn't the resentful type. Seth? Resentful?" she said as though my brother couldn't possibly have any bad thoughts. He was her perfect son, after all.

"I wish we could find that yellow cashmere sweater your brother lost," said my mother. "Every time he's here he mentions it."

"Oh, who *cares* about that sweater!" I said.

"Mr. Joy gave it to him, Jess. He had the sleeve monogramed for Seth. This tiny white *M* is on the right sleeve."

I pushed my chair away from the table. "Who cares about Seth Seth Seth?"

"We had a nice little conversation going for a few minutes," said my mother, "but now I see it's over."

29

THAT AFTERNOON MY mother called up to us, "Jess? Elisa? The parade will be over! You're going to miss Slater Carr's solos! You heard Daddy at lunch, Jess—he's very proud of that boy!"

Only Elisa could answer. "We will be down soon!"

My mother had no way of knowing that upstairs, under Slater Carr's wanted poster, a drama was under way.

"Maybe this was the wrong time to tell you I am going home, but *Vater* announced it at lunch to my aunt, *Mutti*, and me. I go in January. I am still shaken," Elisa said. I could see her hands trembling.

"There's no right time for news that you're going away," I said. "When will you be back?"

"Soon."

"A month? Two?"

"A month. Two. *Süsse*, you don't know all that has happened before this day."

"Whose fault is that? I thought we told each other everything."

"I was too ashamed to tell you."

"What would make you ashamed, Elisa?"

She sat beside me on my bed, atop the Bates bedspread. She held a hanky to her eyes.

"Remember the night we listened to Winchell and then I got the phone call?"

"Yes?"

"You asked me if it was my aunt, and I said it was. But it wasn't."

"Who was it?"

"Wolfgang. He called to tell me they had to rewrite a lot of *Anything Goes* since there was a shipwreck in it. Because of what happened to the *Morro Castle*, they had to cut that out. It would offend too many people. Then he said not to worry, though, because he could still go to Germany."

"You never said he was going to Germany too."

"That was the first I heard either one of us was going there! When he realized I knew nothing about a trip to Germany, he pretended only he was going to visit his grandfather. He said not to worry, he'd be right back."

"I don't understand. Get to what made you ashamed," I said.

I could see our reflection in my bedroom mirror. What

a pair we were! We were dressed as escaped convicts, ankles shackled with leg irons. A month ago I had talked Daddy into getting two old uniforms from the prison basement, the kind with stripes and striped hats to match. At the Halloween parade Elisa and I planned to march in lockstep, the way prisoners were once required to do. Each man walked with arms locked under the man's arms in front of him.

Elisa said, "I was right about Wolfgang paying a lot of attention to me at the party. His father had told him to make friends with me, as a favor to *Vater*."

"Why?"

"Because *Vater* was planning to send *me* to Germany, to bring Omi back. *Vater* knew that as much as I love Omi, I would not want to go. Not even for a few weeks! I am tired of being yanked from schools to go to another place, and this time I did not want to leave because of our friendship."

"I thought your mother was going over there to get her?"

"That was the plan. But *Mutti* hates it so here, my father was afraid she would get to Potsdam and not come back. Omi does not look forward to living here, either. But with *Mutti* still here, there would be a better chance of getting Omi to leave Germany."

"And if Wolfgang Schwitter was traveling there too," I

said, "you would not miss our friendship."

"Please do not rub at it," said Elisa.

"Rub it in," I corrected her, and wished I hadn't.

"*Vater* says all he did was see if Wolfgang planned to visit his grandfather, who is very old. But I know *Vater* talked Mr. Schwitter into sending Wolfgang at the same time I would go. January. *Vater* thought I would like to have a traveling companion."

"Just you and Wolfgang will go?"

"Yes, that is the awful plan."

We both were crying, but the more she talked, the more I wondered what she was really crying about. All right, we would be separated for a while, bad news for me, but she was obsessed with Wolfgang Schwitter. He was all she had been talking about for months.

"Elisa," I said, "you like Wolfgang, don't you? And aren't you coming right back?"

She suddenly had fire in her eyes. "Wolfgang Schwitter has never paid any attention to me before! He never even called me up on the telephone to thank me for giving him Wurst! Remember at the church he forgot my name and called me Phyllis? I reminded him of that at their party. That was when he teased me by dedicating a song to Phyllis. Jessica, he flirted so with me!"

"Maybe he meant it."

"He said that we were going to be a good team. You

see, he already knew then that I was going to Germany, and he would go then too to see his grandfather."

"But the night of the party he didn't try to date you, did he? Didn't you think if he was so attracted to you, he would?"

"No. He was leaving for New York the next day. Before the *Morro Castle* shipwreck the musical would have opened a few weeks from today."

I blew my nose and tried to ignore my mother calling again from downstairs.

I said, "Elisa, I doubt that Wolfgang needed much persuading. You are not like anyone else in Cayuta. You are beautiful, and you are sophisticated."

"I had no friends until you," she said. "I told you I have trouble making friends. And I am *not* beautiful! With my short fingers and arms? You just like me, the same as I like you. You think because I know a few languages that makes me sophisticated? You are naïve, *Süsse*. You saw Wolfgang at the film night. All he cared about was buying the pin Omi gave me. He did not look at me two times after that conversation."

I couldn't think of anything to say to make her feel better. It was just beginning to sink in that she was leaving.

"This is all a maneuver of my father's!" Elisa said. "I am humiliated and ashamed to believe Wolfgang was captured by me. I want nothing to do with anyone forced to like me. I have become suddenly a laughing spot!"

Stock, I said to myself silently.

"Elisa," I said, "you have no reason to be ashamed."

"I have every reason to be ashamed, and I wish I wasn't going. *Vater* knew I would not want to go, not even with Wolfgang to sweeten the journey. Deep in his heart he knew how happy I had become here. That's why *Vater* waited as long as he could to tell me."

"Do you *have* to go?" I said. "Is it an order?"

"Yes, I have to go. That doesn't mean I have to pay any attention to Wolfgang Schwitter! I won't! I will not!"

"Isn't Adolf Hitler supposed to be dangerous?"

"Only if you are Jewish. That's what *Grossmutter* says. Omi says he is good for Germany! She says he is for Germany what Roosevelt is for America!"

"Oh, I hate you to go, Elisa."

It was at that moment the prison sirens rang, louder than the whistle and more persistently. The sirens never rang unless there was a dire emergency.

Running down the stairs, we collided with my mother at the bottom step.

"What are you girls, crazy? Dressing up like that! Are you out of your minds?"

"Why is the prison siren sounding, Mother?" I asked. "Someone couldn't have escaped!"

"No! Someone couldn't have! That is an escape-proof prison now," said my mother. "We haven't had anyone break out up there since your father and I came here!"

The sirens persisted.

Elisa clapped her hands together. "What if it is him?"

"Who?" Mother asked.

"Him. Slater!"

"Elisa, he wouldn't be in the prison with the parade in progress," said my mother. "He'd be downtown."

"Loose," I said.

30

Dear Seth,

You may remember that when I gave you the yellow cashmere sweater a while back, I tried to say how pleased I am to think of you and my beloved J. J. having a future together. I could not pick a better young man for a son-in-law. I know your father from Rotary, and it is my guess that like father like son. Your father and I both are family men, the type who'd rather be walking in the woods with our women than down on a golf course with other men.

Now everyone in Cayuta is at the Halloween parade. Mrs. Joy has gone for lunch-and-a-look with neighbors. J. J. and you have taken our Buick for a picnic at Joyland Park.

Seth, I am no good to my family anymore. Hanging on this way, I am driving them into bankruptcy. We have run through our personal savings and are now about to lose our credit. The only asset I have is my sizable life insurance policy. Gladys and J. J. will not have to worry about money for quite some time.

I remember when I was a young man, slightly arrogant after I inherited the shoe company from an uncle, I had a favorite saying: I clean my own guns. What I meant was I took care of things myself. I didn't depend on others.

It is ironical, because that is what I want this to look like: that I was in the garage, cleaning my guns, and there was an accident. I have only two guns, my Colt .38 from army days and the shotgun I intend for my suicide. I do not want to botch it, for I know that if I do, my family will have to live down the disgrace of an attempted suicide, almost worse than suicide itself.

I am writing to you so that someone close to the Joys will know I did not pick a coward's way out, but a man's only choice: to do what is best for his family. I consider you family, Seth. I never thanked you for getting your father to send an inmate from The Hill (and poor dear Myra as well) to help with the chores. It was so like you to just take charge behind the scenes, assisting us without announcing it.

It is for you to tell J. J. your wish to marry her. I

have not mentioned it to Mrs. Joy or J. J. (named by me Joy! Joy! Joy!—my emotions on her day of birth!). But you know you have my blessings!

Perhaps one day you will share this letter with J. J. Use your own judgment about an appropriate time. I do not believe her mother would welcome this information, for she would feel abandoned by me, but J. J. can decide that.

I am full of memories of the past. Things I used to say and see and sing. There is an old radio here I intend to listen to for a while longer, sit here and smile and hum along. I have every reason to smile, for how happy I have been until these last two years, how I have rejoiced when I would do simple things like come around the corner in my Buick and see this big white house and know that inside, the two people I cherished the most would be waiting to see me. Failure or not, I belong to them, and there is so much love.

That is why I have to do it.

Be strong for J. J., Seth.

Yours, Horace Joy

31

SLATER CARR

WHAT WAS MR. Joy doing? After Slater shoved the jacket of the Blues uniform into a trash can, he watched Joy mail a letter at the corner postbox.

That was news. He hadn't expected him to be home. He was surprised too when Mr. Joy walked to the garage instead of going into the house. Wasn't it late to be going to the parade? Would he have to wrestle him for the Buick?

Slater waited a moment before he followed him into the garage. Inside there was a small radio playing on a table beside an old leather chair with the springs popping.

Mr. Joy did not hear Slater behind him. Slater knew the song playing. "Blue Moon." It was a sad song he had heard over the portable radio the warden had given him, to learn new songs for The Blues' performances. It was about standing alone without a dream in your heart, without a love of your own. Without a car, too, Slater thought ironically. Where was the Buick? And what was Mr. Joy, of all people, doing with two guns?

Never mind. Slater could use one of them. He waited while Mr. Joy sat down in the chair. Then he crept toward him and quickly got him in a headlock with his arm, saying, "Don't move! Just don't move, Mr. Joy!"

"Who're you?" Joy grunted.

"The big bad wolf. How much money do you have?"

At first Slater thought Joy was choking, but he was laughing.

Slater said, "Don't laugh if you want to live. Tell me how much money you can get your hands on!"

"What if I don't want to live?" Joy managed to say.

Slater loosened his hold on the man slightly. "All the more reason to give me your money," he told him.

"Where have I heard your voice before? I know your voice."

"Don't waste my time! I want money!"

"I'm in the process of declaring bankruptcy," Joy said.

"How much loose money do you have?" Slater asked him.

"In my wallet there's about twenty dollars. You've worked around here, haven't you?"

"Don't try to look back. Hand over the wallet."

"I know you. You cut my lawn last week. You're the Bugle Boy."

While Mr. Joy reached behind to his back trousers

160

pocket, Slater lunged for the pistol. Joy reached up and caught the gun's nose and the gun's trigger, and there was the punch of a shot firing. While Joy's body took the shock, his foot knocked the shotgun to the floor, and there was another explosion.

"What did you do?" Slater shouted.

He saw that somehow Joy had shot himself. Joy slumped over and fell to the garage floor. Then Slater saw blood soaking through the yellow sweater he was wearing, the sweater he had swiped from the warden's back porch when he was doing away work there. He had always known he would wear it one day when he found a way out. He had put it on that morning under his Blues uniform.

Slater grabbed the towel Mr. Joy had been using to clean his guns. He wrapped it tightly around himself where the shotgun shot had blasted open his arm down to his elbow.

He had no choice but to leave Joy lying in his own blood on the garage floor near the shotgun and the pistol. Joy's eyes were glazed over like the eyes of a fish at the end of a hook. He was clearly dead.

Slater never would have killed the man. He had actually liked him. Sometimes Joy would come out and work alongside him, weed, paint the trim, whatever he could do to keep himself busy. He hadn't shown the kind of interest in Slater the warden had; he didn't really give a damn for him, though he was probably grateful the boss had sent Slater there some days to help out. But Joy would bring him a cold Coke on a hot afternoon, or a PopSicle from the icebox.

Why hadn't the man just let Slater have the gun?

Why the struggle?

Slater went inside the house, where he had never been. He easily found the phone on the parlor table. The operator took a few moments to get him the number he wanted. It was beginning to get dark out.

"Sir?"

"Who is this?" Slater asked.

"It's the operator, sir."

"Where's my party?"

"Sir? This is hard for me."

"Who are you?"

"My name is Marlene Hellman, sir. I shouldn't even tell a customer my name, but under the circumstances—sir?"

"What? Where's my party?" He was shouting. He would not have any blood left soon. It was running from the towel down his hand, his arms, on his pants, his shoes, on the rug.

"I am sorry to tell you, sir, that your party is deceased."

"No!"

"Yes, sir."

"No! No!"

"I am sorry to say yes, she is deceased, sir. I am sorry."

He hung up and stood there for a few seconds.

Where would the money be hidden in this house, jewelry, anything of value?

Upstairs, he thought. That was where people kept things, hid things.

He saw the winding staircase and took the steps by twos. He was winded and, he realized suddenly, very weak. At the top of the stairs was a huge master bedroom. He headed in there, his heart racing. His back began to ache suddenly, sharp, hard pains, and his gut. Then he had no feeling below his waist.

He fell across the bed.

Although he had never called her Purr to her face, he whispered to himself: "Purr, how could you be dead?"

He lay on his back, on the double bed, tears suddenly filling his eyes and streaming down his face.

She had always been there for him, even after he had gone to prison. The only mail he had ever received had been from her. She had been the only one who had ever loved him.

All he had wanted to do was see her one more time, play with The Georgia Peaches one more time, play "Lord, I'm Coming Home" . . . with feeling.

That was the instant the prison sirens began to wail.

32

"Do you have the radio on, Richard?"

"No. I have a new hat on. A fedora. It cost five bucks!"

"Don't you hear the prison sirens?"

"Is it a Halloween stunt?"

"Slater has escaped. They're looking for him."

"How did he escape?"

"He must have walked away from the parade. When the sirens sounded, Elisa's mother called here and said my father should send a guard to bring Elisa home! Then Elisa just ran out the door, across the street, all the while her mother was telling my mother that obviously my father couldn't control his 'gangsters.'"

"Slater's going to need help, Jessie. He could get himself shot!"

"I knew you'd say something like that. You and Elisa are birds of a feather. She said you should try to find him and get him to go back."

"Yes, but how? *How?*"

"She said take your bike and see if you can find him. He's on foot in that blue band uniform. He knows only a few places. I know that much from Daddy telling me. He did away work at City Hall, our house, and the Joys'."

"Jessie, what if I *do* find him?"

"Elisa says take him a long coat, a cap, some disguise so he can get back safely."

"But why would he want to go back? He just escaped."

"Tell him they'll shoot him dead if he doesn't go back. Elisa says he doesn't want to die."

"How does she know he doesn't want to die?"

"She says he couldn't play like that if he didn't love life."

"I think she's got a crush on him, but so what?"

Once in the summer Elisa had told both Richard and me she might be in love with Slater. I was used to that old line. I knew how she had exaggerated her feelings for him, particularly right after she had heard the bugle. For a while that day, as we'd walked along, Richard had tears in his eyes, even though he'd said to Elisa it must be swell to feel that way about someone. Later he'd told me he'd thought it over and so what if she did love him? He was a lifer, wasn't he?

I said, "Richard? I would help you, but I am not allowed out of the house. I am in the doghouse for dressing up as a convict to go in the Halloween parade. Elisa can't even talk to me on the telephone, her mother's so furious!"

"I just hope some trigger-happy cop doesn't shoot him," Richard said. "I'm going to try to get him on a train."

"No, take him back!"

"Let me handle this my way." Since his braces had been removed, Richard was asserting himself more and more.

I said, "You know what Elisa's mother told me? I called Elisa up to see if the convict costume had gotten her in trouble too, and her mother said I'd never talk to Elisa again!"

"If you want me to find Slater Carr, you'd better let me go right now."

"Did you hear what I just said? Mrs. Stadler said I'd never talk to Elisa again!"

"How's she going to stop you?" Richard said.

"That's what I'd like to know. She said her twin sister was hysterical and Herr Stadler was on his way home from Cornell. All because Slater's running around somewhere."

"You're kidding!"

"She's afraid the whole prison will break out, and she said the Stadlers were not going to live in fear any longer!"

Richard laughed. "I don't believe that woman!" he said.

Later on Richard believed that woman.

We all did.

But late Halloween afternoon Richard went off on his

bicycle to ride through as many neighborhoods as he could. He wore his long raincoat to give to Slater and had even made a small package filled with sandwiches, a Coke, a jackknife, a map of New York State, ten one-dollar bills, nickels for the phone, iodine, and Band-Aids.

Later that night he told me that if he had found Slater, he would even have given his new five-dollar fedora to him, to help with his disguise.

By then we had both heard the news that Slater Carr was dead.

There was no way we could tell Elisa. The Stadlers were not answering phones or doors.

33

BEFORE WE KNEW it, the Stadlers were gone, evacuating with the speed of disaster victims. It had taken them only two days to pack for New York City and book passage on a ship to Germany.

Four days later the postman left a small package in our mailbox addressed to me.

1 November 1934

My dearest best friend ever Jessica,

Aunt Gretchen says Omi is really ill and may even be dying! That was all Vater *had to hear. You know how he loves her. Even if Slater had not made a break, we would probably be going, just not as soon as we are.*

I am so upset that now he is dead, Jessica, and I sail from New York City tomorrow with him a part of the grief I feel. Slater is the first person near my own age who has died and who meant something to me. Even though I never met him, he was part of my life in America, and I will never forget him or the sound of his bugle every night.

I did not know Mr. Joy, so I do not grieve for him, but I guess the whole town does. I believe Slater did not intend to kill him. He would only kill for passion, for love. You told me that.

Mutti *was determined to get us away from that "Wild West" immediately and to keep me from the inevitable sad farewell. She said it was for my own good that I did not see you.*

When I ran from your house still in the prison stripes because so much happened so fast, I forgot what I had on! You can imagine how that was received by my aunt and Mutti!

Inside this package are some things for you. My father is mailing this for me because he knows how much our friendship means to us. Lord Byron, a poet I should have introduced you to, said "Friendship Is Love Without His Wings."

I will write you every chance I get, and you must write me too. I will send you my address the moment I know it. We will not stay with Omi, because she needs a nurse and her house is too tiny. We will return sometime in early January, for

Father has his work at Cornell. Even though Mutti insists we have to relocate to Ithaca, I will see you very often, every weekend. It is not that far from Cayuta.

> *Love and many kisses, dear friend of my life,*
> *Elisa*

P.S. At least Wolfgang Schwitter does not have to be my gigolo now because that was almost what he would have been if he had gone home with me in January. Oh, Papachen *wouldn't have paid him to go with me, but it would have been a favor to Herr Reinhardt Schwitter, so is that not the same thing?*

> *E.*

Inside the package were the dachshund pin and a book of Sara Teasdale's poetry.

34

"WHAT IS PURR doing here?" my father wanted to know
when he came down from The Hill for lunch and saw the
kitten.

"She's been here for over a week," Mother said.
"Mugshot scared her, and she was living under the couch.
Is that your name for her, Purr?"

"I didn't name her."

"I suppose that was the killer's name for her."

"Never mind, Olivia."

"Well, she is called Dietrich now. Mrs. Heinz Pickle
was going to turn her loose in a field somewhere. She said
cats could always get along outside. And *she* is supposed
to be some kind of brain!"

"How did we end up with her?"

"Elisa called Richard Nolan right before they left. She
told Richard the cat was hanging around the Sontags'.

Mrs. Stadler wouldn't let her in. She told the cat to find another place to live. Can you imagine?"

My father shrugged.

Mother said, "If anyone should ride up on a bicycle and ask whose fault all of this is, it's your Mr. Carr's fault! All of it is!"

"It's all my fault," my father said. "I didn't follow the rules."

"Oh, the rules, the rules, Arthur. He was a bad apple."

"I should have perceived that. Horace Joy might be alive today if I had paid closer attention to Mr. Carr's character. Mr. Carr would be too. I got derailed by his musical ability." Then he looked across the table at me and said, "Why aren't you eating?"

"She's still mooning over Miss Germany," said my mother.

In place of any wanted poster on my bedroom wall was an enormous calendar I had made of November and December 1934 and January 1935. I was crossing off the days to whatever date Elisa would return in the first month of the new year.

Daddy had been spending so much time up at the prison, I don't think what was going on anywhere else registered with him. Mother said he was in deep trouble with the authorities because of Slater. He was in so much trouble, she did not even bawl him out for getting the old convict uniforms from the cellar, for Elisa and me to wear on Halloween.

She said, "I still can't believe those Stadlers left without a fare-thee-well, just *pffft* took off, all four."

"You mean all three."

"The twin sister was visiting them from Germany. The grandmother is sick, I heard. They plan to bring her back."

"That's not why they all left, though. They all left because Mrs. Stadler thought there'd be a prison breakout," I said.

"And you two girls were dressed up as convicts!" my mother said. "That might have made *me* leave too, if I had a place to go!"

"I'm sorry, sweetheart." My father tried to smile at me, but the truth was I don't think he could have smiled if his life depended on it. I had never seen him so unhappy. He was hardly ever home, and when he was, he just sat in his chair in the living room and listened to the radio.

He reached over and put his hand on mine for a moment. "I think the Stadlers were unhappy here anyway," he said.

"They're coming back," I said.

"And I'm from Paris, France," my mother said.

"They'll be back in January," I said.

"Well, we'll have to have a celebration for them, complete with party hats."

"Ollie, let up."

My mother said, "Richard Nolan told us the grandmother really is very sick."

"They knew that," I said. "That didn't make them all decide to go at once. Slater Carr loose made Mrs. Stadler a raving maniac."

"Ohhh, shush," said my mother. "Your father feels bad enough."

"You're the one nagging him about it."

"Jess, I don't nag. I am not a nag. If the Stadlers do plan to come back, and I'll believe that when it snows in August, then let's not carry on as though it's their funeral."

"Who said they planned to come back?" my father asked me.

"Elisa said that in her letter."

"So it's not that bad, sweetie."

"How can she come back?" my mother said. "That man won't leave his wife there, and she will *not* come back here! Trust me!"

"He has a job at Cornell!" I insisted.

"That's right, he does," said Daddy. "Where's Seth?"

"At the Joys'," my mother said. "Where else?"

"I still think some sort of service would have been appropriate for Horace Joy."

"Apparently he didn't want one. Seth said it was in his will. Upon his death no memorial of any kind. He was cremated."

My father sighed. "Did Seth say what was in the letter Horace wrote him?"

"He said Mr. Joy gave him permission to marry J. J. when they are graduated."

"Graduated from where?"

"High East, I guess."

"No college?"

"Ask Seth, Arthur. I don't know."

"Why didn't Horace just tell Seth that? Why write a letter?"

"Ask . . . Seth . . . all right?" said Mother. "Have you heard anything from the powers that be?"

"No. The superintendent said the board will meet next month." My dad couldn't eat. He was pushing his chair back from the table, depression visible in his eyes, his shoulders slumped.

My mother followed him down the hall, saying she would give him a massage to relax him. She looked back at me long enough to say, "We may be leaving Cayuta too. Do you realize that, Jess? If your father gets disciplined for what your Goldilocks did, we may be packing up ourselves."

"I don't care," I said. "I don't care about anything."

"Oh, really?" my mother said. "Then why do you ask if there's mail for you the minute you get home from school?"

My father sighed again. He said, "Lay off it, Olivia." Then to me he said, "Mail takes a while, you know. You could wait a month or more."

"If Elisa Stadler writes at all," said my mother. "Don't hold your breath while you're waiting."

PART TWO

November 7, 1934

My dear best friend,

We are experiencing a rough crossing, and poor Mutti *is very sick and cannot wait to be home.*

I will be glad to see my Potsdam again, but also I will eagerly await a return to Cayuta and you, Jessica, knower of all scandalous secrets. Please tell Richard I will write him soon, but probably not until we are there.

I miss our picnics and going to Hoopes Park. I miss our days on Alden Avenue and even at High East, which I hated so at the beginning. I miss you most of all.

Now I wish we could have said auf Wiedersehen, *but* Mutti *was truly afraid of anything or anyone who had something to do with the prison. You know how afraid of our friendship she was and that it would make me admire crime.*

Please for me thank your mother for letting Dietrich stay with you until we are back. It would have been so much more painful to leave worrying about my kitten off in the fields looking for a home. Maybe when I come back, Dietrich and Mugshot will at last be friends. Write please! You may use Omi's address on the back of this envelope.

With love and your eyes in stars,
xxxx Elisa

P.S. I feel bad about our poor Slater. Your father must feel awful too, because wasn't he his pet?

P.P.S. At least I do not have to tolerate Wolfgang Schwitter patronizing me. Apparently he is involved in the opening of that Broadway musical. I forgot the name and the song, but it was something about "your eyes in stars," which gave me the inspiration to sign this that way. I heard he was going to Harvard University but decided to take a year off. Do you see him around Cayuta?

November 29, 1934

Dear Elisa,

 I got your letter today, so by now you are probably in Germany.

I do not feel bad about Slater's death. Slater Carr may have ruined our lives. If the authorities decide to demote my father and send him someplace he cannot have a band, that will be a punishment almost too hard for my father to bear. If he is fired or sent to another prison, I will have to live somewhere else and be gone by the time you get back.

I just don't get it. Why would Slater do such a thing after my father was so good to him? I liked poor Mr. Joy too, but I still cannot stand J. J.

Something strange is going on here, which I can't figure out.

The other night Daddy came home very late, held up by a meeting of the prison board. Of all things, Seth was waiting up for him, and they went into the living room to talk. The two of them haven't just sat and talked for almost a year. All I could hear was this:

—Dad? I've been waiting for you.

—Is everything all right, Seth?

—Do you know about the letter?

—The one from Horace Joy?

—Yes.

—Giving you permission to marry J. J.?

—Can we talk about it, Dad?

—Of course. Come into the living room.

Come into the living room, where I can't hear anything from the stairs. And they shut the door! We never shut the living room door. So that is a big mystery. You should have heard Seth's voice. As you would say, he sounded full of bash.

One thing I did not think that much about until I got your letter. Yes, you are right: My father must feel terrible about Slater's death. It might bring Seth back to him, but I think (and don't quote me) my father was fonder of Slater. I know that sounds just awful, but when you think about it, a father has to be fond of his son, but my father picked Slater out of everyone on The Hill and gave him a radio and all that away time. Now I see better, thanks to you, why he is so down in the dumps. I have never seen him this way before. Yes, his job is on the line, but that isn't news. He was always being bawled out for being too lenient with the prisoners. This time, though, he is a basket case. Don't ask me to translate that. Just trust me, he's in bad shape!

I did a paper on Sara Teasdale, which I am sending you. Tell me what you think of it. Miss Hightower wanted to know if I knew what became of Sara Teasdale. I said she killed herself, and Miss Hightower said why would you pick someone who did that? I said I didn't pick her because of that, but what was wrong with killing yourself if life is unbearable? She said if life was unbearable you should learn to have faith in God. I told her what you once said to me: that I would like to believe in God, but I would wait until there was more proof. I should have told her I used to think of doing what Sara did. Remember the time we talked about it and you said everyone had suicidal thoughts? That was the last of them for me. That feeling is gone now. Who wants to be like everyone? Besides, I hope to see YOU again, soon, I hope.

I am doing a lot of reading, mostly poetry, which I am beginning to like, and for a combined early Christmas/ birthday gift I am sending you Edna St. Vincent Millay's collected works with my composition on Teasdale. Millay is my favorite as of this moment.

I will keep writing. You must too. Does your father say when you are coming back?

Love and kisses, Jessica

P.S. Guess who sleeps with my mother at night? Dietrich! At last she has someone!

P.P.S. I do not see any of the Schwitters around town. That does not mean they aren't here. We just don't *run into each other. Do you still think of Wolfgang that way?*

December 16, 1934

My dearest best friend, Jessica,

When we arrived in Germany, we stayed with Omi in the small village outside Potsdam where I grew up. We were not prepared for the signs we saw along the road as we entered.

JUDEN UNERWÜNSCHT! Jews unwanted!

That was mild for what was ahead. I wish you knew more German, because the words sound so much harsher to my ears, but I will translate.

THOSE WITH HOOK NOSES AND KINKY HAIR SHALL NOT ENJOY OUR LAND!

WHO HELPS THE JEWS HELPS COMMUNISTS! GERMANY! WAKE UP! GET RID OF JEW TRAITORS!

Omi says it is a temporary thing and not to pay attention. I guess she is right, for there are more pleasant surprises, and it is not all so bad here. You should see the roads! There are no billboards advertising things and no food stands, no telephone poles, no gas stations. Trucks are not allowed either.

The roadsides are planted with shrubs and trees, and grass strips divide the two ways of traffic, all kept immaculately.

I will write you in more detail when I have time, for we are looking for an apartment in Berlin. Mother thinks Omi is too ill to travel just now, and she must be out of her house next month. Do not worry, because I intend to return to America with Father. I will be company for Papachen, *and we will be back across the street at least until school is out. He does not now mention finding a house nearer Cornell either, plus we have paid the Sontags rent already for months ahead.*

How is Dietrich? I hope your mother will not be too fond of her, so when we return, I will be able to retrieve her.

Please tell Richard I think of him often and will write him when we get settled. Now, I write only you. My father said Richard could have been arrested for aiding the escape of a prisoner if he had found Slater that day. I love Richard for that.

I understand that you can't forgive Slater. I believe he was trying for his freedom and was caught attempting to steal Mr. Joy's car. Vater says the gunfight that ensued killed them both. Do you know any more about the letter Mr. Joy wrote to Seth? What could he have said?

I regret so much that your father is blamed for giving Slater too much freedom. I believe that is what life is all about: being free.

Today I am sixteen! Beethoven too had his birth-day today.

With much love, stars, your friend always, Elisa

P.S. Your package did not arrive yet. Mail is slow here.

Elisa dearest,

New Year's Eve at the stroke of midnight I made a wish you would come back next month.

Everyone in school is excited that I got mail from Europe! My father is interested in what you have to say about how Jews are treated. He says it is hard to believe and that you must be in a small enclave where there is anti-Semitism. He remem-bers when he went to a wardens' convention in Miami, Florida, last year there were certain hotels with "Restricted" on their signs outside. That means no Jews. That must be how it is where your grandmother lives. There must be many places that do not have those feelings, just as we do not have restricted hotels up north and the colored can use public bathrooms. (They can't in our south, did you know that?)

My father says he stopped himself from saying he "Jewed someone down" when he realized it was offensive, even though it is not an uncommon expression for getting a bargain. My mother says there are many Jews she likes (her own doctor is one) but not living on our street because it brings down property values.

I don't think I have ever been friends with a Jew, but I certainly would not mind that.

The prison board meeting was postponed to next month, and we will know then if Daddy will remain in Cayuta or what. If it weren't for you, I would be praying he gets sent back to Elmira. Daddy was the one who got the band started there, and though they never won a Baaa, one year they came in second.

I don't think I will ever know what Mr. Joy wrote to Seth. But Seth is acting completely different toward my dad. They both are acting different. I said to Seth, "What's going on with you and Dad?

Anyone would think you're father and son."

He didn't think it was funny, I guess. He pretended not to hear. One night out of the blue Seth said to me that one thing neither of us should ever do is underestimate Dad. I told Seth I never did, did he? He said he thought everyone underestimated our father.

My mother notices them too but says they are close again because Slater Carr is out of the picture. Did I ever tell you she can't say the word dead? She says "out of the picture, passed, crossed over," anything but!

There is a writer I think you would like called Sinclair Lewis. Richard is very excited about him too and says Babbitt is the story of our parents' hypocrisy. The main character, George Babbitt, sells people houses for more than they can afford to pay.

Richard says our parents are all conniving snobs. He says we overvalue them just because they are our parents. I don't think my father is a bad man, but I can see why Richard thinks that, since his father takes people's cars away if they miss a payment. When I finish Babbitt, he says, I can send it to you.

We had a very quiet Christmas. We had the usual

tree indoors, but Mother did not think we should decorate outdoors because of Mr. Joy and also because Daddy's fate is still undecided.

Please tell me what you are reading, and if it is in English, I can read it too. I would like to compare notes with you. I think you will be surprised at what a big poetry reader I am becoming. My teachers can't believe it. They say they believe my friend from Germany made me more appreciative of it, and I say they are right!

Please write me often, as I will you.

Love and xxxxx, Jessica

P.S. Daddy is still sad and in the dark about what will become of him (and us).

P.P.S. Do you ever think of Wolfgang? I never see him anywhere.

February 1, 1935

Dearest best friend Elisa,

You will not believe this. This morning as I was dressing for school I listened to our local station.

They play all the latest hits, and lo and behold on came the song with "your eyes in stars above" in the lyrics. I'm sure that's the song Wolfgang sang to you—"The Very Thought of You."

After school Richard and I went down to Dare's Music Shop and listened to the song and copied the words down so you could have them. They are enclosed. I remember you said how you liked that song, even though you didn't like the idea of your father trying to fix you up with Wolfgang. You probably would still have your eye on him if it weren't for that, I bet.

I heard Wolfgang did not go to Germany yet but is planning a visit there. My mother heard it from the Schwitters' maid, who is the wife of one of our guards. I never do see much of him.

I just want to rush this off to you.

Xxxxxx come back soon . . .

Your dearest friend,
Jessica

P.S. Richard has a "push" on a German writer called Friedrich Nietzsche, and he is always quoting him. One line he quoted is when Nietzsche said, "As an artist, a man has no home in Europe save in Paris." Now I would give anything to be in Paris with you, and I would go up in the elevator too.

Richard thinks he will be a writer and go there to live.

February 28, 1935

Dearest friend Jessica,

At times America, and Cayuta, seem far away, as though it were a long time ago that I was there. But here I am in Germany, and my poor country seems almost as distant and unreal.

Jessica, do you remember once we had a conversation about your mother wanting your neighborhood Judenrein? Remember that word? Jew free . . . There is a growing feeling in so many places now that Jews are the cause of all our troubles and that we should get them out of Germany. Now the signs against them are everywhere and get uglier every day. Your father is wrong to think it is just in one part of this country. I don't think Americans know what is going on here.

I went with Vater to the All-German Farm Festival in the Harz. It is a major celebration in Germany. Farmers from all over assemble. We were invited to stay overnight with old friends of our family. With us were a man and wife, also friends of my father, the Schulzes, prosperous farmers from Hessen. We were having dinner when the eight-year-old daughter of our hosts refused to take a platter of sauerkraut and sausage from Mrs. Schulze. This little girl, blond, blue-eyed, and "cute" you would call her, in her school uniform, blue skirt, white blouse, shouted out, "I am forbidden to take anything from a Jew nose's hands!" Then, shaking her tiny fist at Mr. Schulze, she cried, "Jew, you and your wife, leave our German house!"

Everybody was embarrassed for our hosts, who apologized profusely, and a servant then passed the food, stopping by each guest to offer some. The little girl, Gudrun, was sent to her room. You would think that would be enough of a picture for you to see what it is like here, but no! The next day the servant was arrested and taken away. Gudrun reported her.

Even if you are not Jewish, you feel the fear in Germany. Life goes on with crowds attending opera and theater. Jews cannot go to public events, cannot go to concerts or perform in them, cannot even sit in public parks. And then suddenly you see a Jew being shamed in public by a Nazi officer, or you hear of one whose windows were painted over with swastikas, the Nazi emblem.

Mother says because growing up I have lived so many places, I do not know and trust my homeland as she and my Omi do. They say this will stop.

We are probably going to rent an apartment in Berlin. I am not certain when we can return. It is not easy to come and go now, but my father says not to worry because he must continue with his work at Cornell.

So everything is postponed a little, and everything will be better soon, I keep hearing. Only my father does not say that. He does not say much, for he is too shocked, I think. I believe he is expecting Wolfgang and Mr. Schwitter to arrive here soon. He says he wrote warning them it is a bad time for anyone to visit Germany. What about us? I said to him, and he said that is different because this is our home. I don't remember its being this way, and Vater said it wasn't this way ever and it won't be for long.

It is peculiar that I miss Dietrich, because I did not have her long, but she made an impression, the same as you did, on my heart. My mother says when we settle down in Berlin, I can get a kitty, and she will take care of it while I return to America. She may not come when I do because it may take a long

*time before Omi is strong enough. Everyone is doing
all they can to make me like it here, but I do not feel
it is my Germany, and I miss you so!*

     With love and stars from your friend, Elisa

*P.S. No longer can you greet or say good-bye to
someone with the customary* Grüss Gott. *Now you
must say* Heil Hitler*! Everything you say and do
gets reported to police.*

P.P.S. Remember me by being nice to a Jew.

March 9, 1935

My dearest friend Elisa,

     *You do not mention the package I sent you for
your birthday/Christmas celebration. I hope it did
not get lost in the moving.*

     *There is some good news, some bad. Daddy did
not get a demotion. He did not get a year-end bonus
either, but he said with the times the way they are,
he might not have gotten one anyway.*

     *The bad news is he cannot have a band at the
prison, not even one that remains in the prison and*

is never allowed outside its walls. This makes him very discouraged, because the music was always a morale booster for the inmates. (And Daddy too.)

He says that it is his own fault. I tell him that it is all the fault of Slater Carr. He says, "Maybe we can't forget some things, but we can forgive them. After all, Mr. Carr had a life he missed. That was my mistake, Jess, thinking he had no one and would adjust to The Hill. But everyone has a life of some sort."

Seth feels bad that Mrs. Joy has moved all the way to St. Louis, Missouri, where she has a sister! Of course J. J. had to go with her. Seth would travel there for Easter vacation, but we do not have the money, says Daddy. Not for that, he says, so Seth has taken an after-school job at Hollywood Hangout, and also an early-morning job delivering The Cayuta Advertizer. *Mother is very proud of him. She would like nothing better than to see her son marry a "shoe Joy," as she calls J. J.*

Please let me know about the package. I can send another.

I am reading Goodbye, Mr. Chips *by James Hilton for English. You would like it, I think. It is about a beloved schoolmaster like your Kai (I forgot his last name), who got you to read* Les Misérables.

I wonder what you do daily. Can you give me an idea?

The only thing new about my day is that now I write you and also sometimes even hear from you (Hint! Hint!).

> *Love from your best friend in the world!*
> *Jessica*

March 23, 1935

Dearest Elisa,

Now I will tell you something amazing. Last night Daddy took me for a walk to Hollywood Hangout. I can count on one hand the times we have gone for a walk together, so I knew he was going to say something important. I never dreamed he would say what he said.

What he said was that my mother had one lung removed when we moved here because she had gotten tuberculosis! It was not the pneumonia that she was always talking about at all. It had to be this big secret because by law she would have had to go to a sanitarium since it is a contagious disease. Instead Daddy decided to keep her home and to keep it between themselves and a doctor in Rochester. She could not tell a single soul for fear news would get out and she would be sent away. She would never have told anyone anyway, since she was so ashamed, believing (wrongly) that only lower classes get it.

Over the Fourth of July on her regular visit to Rochester, the doctors told my mother if her next checkup bears it out, she no longer has TB! Well, she doesn't.

That makes everything clearer, doesn't it? I now know why she coughed so much, why Daddy took her walking every day, and why she kept her distance from me. No wonder I never saw them embrace anymore. They always seemed so frigid to me, particularly when across the street on the Sontags' porch were the lovebirds.

Think of all the times I said they weren't doing it, and you said they had to be doing it. No wonder poor Daddy got obsessed with winning the Baaa. He'd always wanted to win it, but after we got here, it seemed like all he thought about . . . and then his attachment to Slater came. Slater would make his dream come true!

I have promised Daddy you are the only one I will tell. He does not even want me to tell my mother I know. She is still humiliated and still believes only poor, uneducated people get TB. She was always so terrified someone would look down on her. After Daddy told me this, all I could think of was all the dirty books she kept under her mattress. I guess because she couldn't do it with Daddy. And of course that explains the sleeping porch and why they weren't lovey-dovey and why I thought she was an icicle.

When I say it explains almost everything, it doesn't explain why she couldn't cough up a few words of affection now and then. That part makes me mad! It also makes me determined to always let the people I love know it. No matter what happens in life, we should always show our feelings, I think.

You have helped me be able to do this, in case anyone should ride up on a bicycle and ask you, as my mother would say. Before you came along, I was this drip who couldn't find words to express myself, particularly sentimental ones. That's probably why I didn't take to poetry, which now is #1.

My feelings about you, besides love, are anxious ones. Even though Daddy says you can get over things, that you must to go on, I will never get over thinking about you and hoping that you're okay. Not a day goes by that I don't wonder what you're

doing. *Is your family well? Please, please write,*
Elisa.

Your friend forever, Stars,

Jessica

P.S. You never mention Wolfgang anymore. How
come?

✦ ✦

March 22, 1935

Dearest Jessica,

    Thank you for the fudge, but I must tell you
something about packages. I did not receive yours
for a long while, which is why I said nothing, fearing
it was lost. Then came a notification from customs
that a box addressed to me contained a book and a
paper forbidden entry to the Reich.

    Dear friend, you must understand this is a
time of reorganization in Germany and there are
controls. Most books you would send would be
censored as the Millay one was and a paper like
the one about Teasdale too. Do not send your
Sinclair Lewis either. Send nothing! I will not get
it. It is best not to send me packages of any kind,

and I will not send you any.

I must make this short.

Xxxx Elisa

P.S. You ask me always about Wolfgang Schwitter. You sound sometimes like Mutti *worrying that I will never have a* Verlobter. *Even if he was here, I do not have time for boys.*

April 19, 1935

Dearest Elisa,

Our letters crossed and I'm afraid I sent you some more books and fudge without knowing I wasn't supposed to.

Have you moved to Berlin? Your last letter was just a note. I was so worried that I called the Schwitters to ask when Wolfgang and his father would be going there and have they plans to see you and your family? Mrs. Schwitter invited me to a spring vacation party she was giving for Dieter's friends from Paris Arts & Science and Miss Thacker's School for Girls. I actually enjoyed myself! It was then that she told me Mr. Schwitter and

Wolfgang will perform soon in Berlin. They were in New York City making arrangements. She said they would probably see you at some point. Wolfgang wants to live in New York City when he returns and try his luck with theater.

I took Richard with me. He always claimed he did not like what he calls "big society parties," but he behaved so well. When we were going home, he asked me if I really liked Dieter, as I seemed to, or if I was just being nice to him to remember you. I did really, really like him. He is not high hat or anything you would think a Schwitter could be. But I didn't understand this remark of Richard's.

I said, "What does being nice to Dieter have to do with Elisa?"

"Didn't she tell you to be nice to a Jew? She did me."

"Dieter is not a Jew, silly."

"Before I went there tonight," said Richard, "my father told me he saw Reinhardt Schwitter once in a men's room, and he was circumcised. He said he had also heard somewhere that Schwitter was born Jewish. Doesn't that make Dieter a Jew? And Wolfgang?"

I said, "I don't believe you! Why would Mr. Schwitter buy the town a Christmas tree every year?"

Richard said, "Because he's not religious. My father was born Catholic, but have you ever seen him at Holy Family? Not all religious people stay religious, and I don't think Dieter or Wolfgang ever were."

What do you think of that?

I remember you told me Jews in Germany now couldn't go to concerts or perform, but the Schwitters are going to perform there, so I think Richard's father has wrong information. When I told my mother what Richard said, she said Richard was crazy! She said of all people to accuse of being Jewish, the Schwitters were the most unlikely.

When do you think you'll be heading back?

My mother is practically swooning over the idea I know Dieter because he is a Schwitter. He calls me just to talk sometimes, not about anything in particular, about anything that comes to our heads. He's an intellectual like you, only he is very serious and worried about Germany. Seth calls him "the likable Schwitter."

I know you probably still think of Slater, and I don't want you to keep from mentioning his name because I have trouble forgiving him for what he did. But have you thought about the way everything changed because of him? You might still be *in America, and my poor father might still be in charge of The Blues, if Slater hadn't escaped. At night I trace everything way back to my own blame in this. I never should have told you all the stories about the prisoners and how Daddy liked murderers to work at our house. You went and told your mother, and she got more and more afraid. Did you ever think that if I hadn't done that, maybe Slater would have kept on doing his away work in our yard? Then Daddy would never have sent him to the Joys'. He wouldn't have even known where they lived.*

I have never told anyone about Daddy's helping the Joys out that way. Mother must have agreed with the idea, since she sent Myra over too.

If Daddy had sent some other inmate to work there, Mr. Joy would still be alive. Slater might even still be loose. So here and now I want to apologize for my big part in all this trouble. Could God be punishing me for this by keeping you in Germany? I don't think I even believe in God. There's so much trouble in the world, if He is there, why doesn't He do something about it?

Are you in school or what? You say you don't have time for boys, so what do you do? I can't envision your day. What is it like? I am studying

Spanish in school. They don't teach German, or I would take that.

Hasta luego and yo te amo, Jessica. Stars! Write!

P.S. Send a photograph before I forget what you look like. I am having some film developed, so I will send you one too.

June 3, 1935

Dear Jessica,

Yes, Wolfgang and Herr Schwitter are in Berlin. They will both be in the all-Mendelssohn concert given by the Jüdischer Kulturbund *this week. Herr Reinhardt Schwitter will play the solo part in the violin concerto. Only Jews can attend, and only music by Jewish composers can be played. No Aryan music allowed! I am so disappointed, because I love Mendelssohn and I would like to hear the Schwitters play too.*

My father said he simply forgot Reinhardt Schwitter was a Jew, if he ever knew it at all. He said Germans have never paid attention to that until recently. Now it seems Judaism is not considered a religion but a race. No one has a choice to say they are or are not Jewish. It is a fact, on record.

No, it is not easy for them, Jessica, they are not a popular race in Germany today. Of course I did not have an inkling the Schwitters are Jews. My mother cannot believe it.

I have seen Wolfgang only one time on the street, then only long enough to tell him how sorry I was that Wurst had to be suddenly taken. Jews can no longer have pets. Without warning they were taken away.

Jessica, I do not know when we will come back, but it will not be this summer.

It is nobody's fault.

Of course I am disappointed, but I cannot always have my own way.

With much love,
Elisa

P.S. Do not feel that you have to write so much to me. I have no time to answer. Then I feel bad. Notice Berlin address, but do not put your name on the return address. By now I know from whom the letter comes.

September 14, 1935
Arts & Science Academy
Paris, New York

Dear Jessie,

How good it was to see you last weekend. I never used to look forward to going home for weekends, but now I do, and it is all because of you. I must say there is no one I talk with so easily. I wonder if you noticed that about us.

I know you probably want news of Elisa, so I am enclosing three pages of Wolfgang's latest. This letter will probably explain, too, why I made no effort to call you this week. As you can imagine, I am not in a mood to talk. None of this has been told to the newspapers because my mother fears reprisals if it got out that we are trying to make an incident of what is happening there. We have other means of communicating with family and friends who know more about the political climate in Germany.

Last month my father was taken away for sitting and talking with Mr. Stadler on a park bench.

Stadler too was grabbed, but not put in the truck my father went into with others who had made various "mistakes." Aryans are not allowed to sit with Jews anywhere in public and vice versa. We do not know what became of Mr. Stadler. We are concerned for Father, for he may have been shipped off to the mysterious "unknown destination" with other Jews.

They have wanted Father for a long time but waited until the Jüdischer Kulturbund *Mendelssohn concert was over. My father was a feather in Propaganda Minister Joseph Goebbels' hat. Not only did the* Kulturbund *make it look to the world as though the Reich is not abusive to the Jews, but also they boasted there was the famous musician Reinhardt Schwitter, who came from America to star in its concert!*

There is no word about my father. Jews are whisked away for any small infraction of rules and sometimes never seen again. Or they are simply grabbed from the streets for no reason. This is particularly true of ones they suspect are Communists or professionals like teachers, doctors, etc. Even if someone is just too brilliant to suit them (a Jew should not be brilliant!), it is enough. They take away (to God knows where) anyone from a poor tailor to a university professor or a rich manufacturer.

Certain Aryans disappear too, particularly friends of Jews.

I will call you soon when I know the next week-end I can come home.

Sincerely,

Dieter

Please send back the pages of Wolfgang's letter. They are for your eyes only.

(ENCLOSED)

(p.3) and I feel ashamed to write of missing Wurst, but he was like family. No one knows what became of the pets. One can only hope they were killed instantly, but more likely they were sold somewhere, for a lot were pedigreed dogs and cats. Sometimes they were thrown out windows or collars they wore were tightened until they choked. Anyone who had a fish or bird: Fish were dumped in street, and birds hung by their necks out the windows on strings.

I saw Elisa Stadler at the Stadler apartment for a short time just days before Father and Mr. Stadler were taken. Father and I had gone there to discuss giving Grandfather's Beckstein piano to Mrs. Stadler. She did not even dare accept the gift for fear of looking as though she had strong ties with us. Too bad, for soon came the SS to snoop around Grandfather's house, and they threw that beautiful instrument out the third-floor window. They like to throw things out windows!

(p.4) Elisa behaved so strangely. I always felt we were slightly attracted to each other, that in the right circumstances we could have become friends. When our father asked me if I would like to visit Germany in January, ahead of schedule since he and I were going over in spring, I was so pleased to hear I would be company for Elisa on the crossing and look out for her there. At our party last summer I sang "The Very Thought of You." I looked directly at her. I was sure she felt that. I also called her from New York once, but midway in the conversation she became cold and cut it short. I don't know what I said or even if it was something I said.

Then Fate intervened, and it was some time before I saw her again. Once, here on the street. She was with others but stopped to say she was sad about Wurst. The second time, at her family's apartment, Elisa was remote and spoke little to me. She asked me if I thought Myrer sounded like a Jewish name to Germans. I said Jews spelled that name Meyer, usually, but who knows what a postal inspector would make of it? I think she was receiving packages from Jessie Myrer and was worried that postal inspectors were watching her mail. Then she abruptly ended our conversation by leaving the room without a word to me.

Mrs. Stadler said Elisa had gone to her old school expressly to say hello to a schoolmaster named Kai Kahn. He had just then been made to clean the street with his beard by a contingent of SS men. The incident was in progress. Mrs. Stadler said Elisa was very upset by it, and she offered it as an excuse for the sullen way Elisa received me.

(p.5) She may be genuinely worried and afraid. You don't have to be a Jew to worry about what will happen next. Our grandfather's maid of twenty-two years was told she could not work anymore for Grandfather since she is an Aryan. They are not allowed to work in the house of a Jew or even serve a Jew in a café. I don't know where Martha will find work, and I don't know how Grandfather will manage without her. He is so weak now, and she

was the only one who could coax him to eat. They were like father and daughter. She cannot even visit him, for it is against the rules to go to a Jewish house.

Do not tell all of this to Mother. She is worried enough as it is and even threatens to join us. She must not! Even though she knows it is dangerous, she wants to be with Father. Please don't you get any heroic ideas about accompanying her. Don't ask for trouble, Dieter!

October 10, 1936

Dear Elisa,

ARE YOU ALL RIGHT?

Please just let me know that much if you can't tell me more.

I am so worried about you!

Have a heart!

Love, Stars, Memories, Jessica

January 3, 1936

Dear Jessica,

The Reich wishes everyone to have the experience of Arbeitsdienst, *which translates as "work service," soon to become compulsory for girls. I already volunteered and will be assigned to a camp with factory workers. It will be good for me, and healthy.*

I have learned a lot about my homeland that I did not realize, particularly how unfairly we were treated by the Versailles Treaty in 1919. Germany was forced to pay the Allies an enormous amount of money; hand over all our colonies; accept full blame for the war; reduce the size of our military; and give land outright to Belgium, France, Denmark, and Poland.

The map of Europe was redone, and we were forced into the Great Depression, which would make your own little depression insignificant! We were being punished for the war as though it were solely our fault.

Hitler understood the feeling of humiliation and betrayal all Germans harbored. He alone has restored our pride!

I never knew anything about this part of our history! I don't think it was taught in any school I attended, for how could I forget such treachery!

It makes me ashamed of myself for knowing all my various languages and quotations from literature but nothing about my own people and how they suffered. I was such a dilettante!

Jessica, I now belong to the League of German Girls. In German Bund deutscher Mädel. *I enclose a photograph of me in my uniform.*

See how proud I look. It is because I am dedicated to Germany, and my entire ardor will henceforth go into her service.

You may be surprised, my friend, for when we knew each other, I was so ignorant and uncaring of anyone but myself. That is all past. I say auf Wiedersehen *and wish you a productive and meaningful 1936!*

Sincerely,
Elisa Stadler

February 10, 1936
Arts & Science Academy
Paris, New York

Dear Jessie,
Your note with enclosed letter from Elisa Stadler

just arrived. I wish I could be of help with regard to Elisa Stadler. My brother has not seen her since last fall, nor does he have any news of Mr. Stadler. As you know, our own father is in a concentration camp called Dachau, outside Munich, but we do not hear from him. We only heard that he was there from someone who was released.

There are not many people released from these places. There is never anything about them in the newspapers, there or here. In case you don't know, they are horrible places with guards and barbed-wire fences, and prisoners are taken there in airless, crowded trains. We hear rumors about them in the few letters that can be smuggled out of Germany. Guards make people work long hours in nearby factories, without pay or any consideration for their health. They routinely murder people without cause. No, there is not much about this in any newspapers. Eyes shut when it comes to Germany and what is happening to the Jews.

My mother and I are expecting Wolfgang home this spring. Grandfather is so near death, he cannot last much longer.

If Elisa is proud to be a member of the League of German Girls, she has become a convert to the

Third Reich. I shook my head when I read what you wrote about being surprised she would join them, since she always said she would never join a sorority. Jessie, forget the Elisa you knew. Her letter is telling you that. If I were you, I would forget that friendship too. If you persist in writing to her, it is best not to mention names of people. That can cause them big trouble if her letters are being censored.

I hope we can get together a lot during spring vacation. My family is not having any parties this year, as you can understand. But I have a better time with just you and me anyway.

Pray that by then we have Wolfgang home and some good news about my papa and Mr. Stadler too. I'll call you soon.

Yours, Dieter

THE CAYUTA ADVERTIZER

MARCH 10, 1936

FORMER RESIDENT DEAD

The American Red Cross reports that Professor Heinz Stadler, a visiting professor at Cornell University, died as the result of an accident in Munich, Germany, in December 1935.

Dr. Stadler and his wife, Sophie Stadler, and their daughter, Elisa, lived for a while on Alden Avenue in the house belonging to Thomas and Gertrud Sontag.

Heinz Stadler's expertise was in agriculture, and he was learning hydroponics in Ithaca with the intention of teaching this new method of plant growing at the University of Heidelberg.

Elisa was a student at Cayuta High East, and the family were communicants at Holy Family Church.

The Stadlers had returned to Germany to bring back Mrs. Stadler's mother. Recent political upheaval delayed them. Then Professor Stadler's death canceled the return plans.

March 11, 1936

Dearest Elisa,

We have word here of your father's death. There are no words I can find to tell you how sorry I feel, how much I think of you going through such sadness.

We are reading Romeo and Juliet *in school now. You've probably read it, but I never have, and I am so surprised by its power. For instance, if something happened to someone I loved, I would have this for an epitaph:*

When he shall die,
Take him and cut him out in little stars,
And he will make the face of heaven so fine
That all the world will be in love with night,
And pay no worship to the garish sun.

It is interesting how stars figure into things with us. The song you heard Wolfgang sing that summer night, which seems so long ago, is always coming over the radio, reminding me of you and a time when we weren't so out of touch.

I hope you will remember something always: I am not a fair-weather friend. Do you have that expression in German? It means I am not there for you just in good times, and just when we agree on things, and just when we are near each other.

Elisa, when you wrote me telling me how proud you are to be a member of the League of German Girls, I was so delighted, not because I know anything about that group but because you trusted me enough to tell me how you feel about Germany. You may think I can't understand your new feelings about your country. What I can understand is that the League is something you care dearly about, so of course I want to know more without you having any fear we won't think alike. What if we don't?

I never became friends with you because you believe Les Misérables *is such a wonderful book. Do you want to know the truth? I had to plow through it! I always copy passages from books I read, but I copied only one from this book by Hugo: "The supreme happiness of life is the conviction that we are loved."*

I don't even think that's very profound or original, but it was all I could find in the book to mark. The other thing is: I didn't care that much for Jean Valjean. It's probably because of Slater

Carr. Reading it, I did think of him in his "blues" with the B cap, and with his angel face, but not any longer with sympathy or fondness. So you see, we do not think alike maybe, but you are and will always be my only dear friend.

I wish when you suffer any unhappiness, you can feel my concern and trust that no matter what happens in the years to come—even if we lose track of each other—I am still for you, no matter what.

I think of lazy days we "lollygagged" about in our iron swing on the front porch, talking about every-thing and talking about nothing.

I really miss you, Elisa. I am sorry about your Papachen.

If you don't want me to write, just say so. Please don't.

All stars are ours.

Love, Jessica

P.S. Remember Dieter? He comes home weekends from A&S often. We take long walks in Hoopes Park. He does not act at all like his brother. He is full of bash and quiet.

April 16, 1936
Arts & Science Academy
Paris, New York

Dear Jessie,

The enclosed is for you from my brother. I'll call you when I get home the weekend after next.

Yours, Dieter

(ENCLOSED)

Dear Jessica,

Knowing your interest in Elisa Stadler, I am asking Dieter to pass this on to you.

I saw Elisa several weeks ago in downtown Berlin. I saw her, I thought, before she saw me, and I had no intention of compromising her by speaking to her. A Jew doesn't walk up to a member of the League of German Girls and say Howdy!

I begin to understand why she wasn't friendly before. She doesn't want to jeopardize her reputation in her new "sorority."

Those girls were busy taking down all the insulting signs about Jews, which are everywhere in this city. No, there has not been a change of heart in this country. The signs will go right back up as soon as the Olympics are over. Hitler does not want Germany to look like Germany when the foreigners arrive for their sports games. Guests of the Third Reich may have heard a little about the persecution of Jews, but there will be no sign of that (no signs!) thanks to dedicated daughters of Hitler like your friend Elisa. . . . I can remember when I was slightly under her spell, but she is not that young woman anymore.

I was wrong to think she hadn't seen me, for she had. She looked right at me as they marched by, or should I say she looked right through me? I have never seen anyone with such cold eyes. Yes, I was undoubtedly a threat to her, but there are ways to let someone know that. She could have told me when we were there about the piano. On the street she could have winked, given me a sign, something, but she is a bona fide Nazi, I'm afraid.

I am sorry to tell you this, Jessica, for I know you were dear friends with her, but I advise you to put her out of your thoughts.

I am sending all of this correspondence through a friend who is leaving the country and can mail this somewhere else. We do not send letters from here for fear they will be opened and never reach their destinations.

I would also advise you not to write to her if she is not writing to you. It will not help her to receive mail from a foreigner, particularly one from the U.S.

Although my grandfather died a month ago, I remain here hoping for news about Father. We know he is in the concentration camp, but all reports from places like Dachau are hearsay. You may have been informed that Elisa's father was killed in Dachau, but of course there are no details.

Sincerely,
Wolfgang Schwitter

EPILOGUE

FOR TEN YEARS I thought of Elisa, wondering what happened to her and if I would ever see her again. After America entered the war in 1941, we learned more about this Hitler and his idea of a master race. We made fun of him in jokes and songs, never truly comprehending what his "final solution" meant until we saw photographs of our troops liberating what was left of the Jews and other captives of the concentration camps. On my desk blotter, up in the corner, I have still the photo Elisa sent me of herself in the uniform of the League of German Girls. I have all her letters, of course, including the last one, in which she announced that Hitler had restored Germany's pride and wished me a happy 1936, presumably her goodbye to me. Although I wrote her for a while after that, she never answered, and finally my letters were returned "address unknown."

Dieter Schwitter told me that his brother refused to talk about Germany. Wolfgang told him he preferred to let the theater take him to fantasy land forever; he would not look back. Unlike Wolfgang, Dieter vows to dedicate his life to studying the Holocaust, and he is already finishing his doctorate on that subject.

It seemed that small but ever-so-important part of my growing up, making my first friend and my first acquaintance with someone from another country, would never have a conclusion and would always remain a mystery to me.

Then, out of the blue, one day I had word of Elisa again. It came to me in a letter from her mother, addressed to the Alden Avenue house the prison still provided for my father.

September 3, 1946

Dear Jessica,

In 1944 I married a violinist I met in Paris, where I have lived since 1943. In summers, we come to the Languedoc in southern France, where we have a small villa.

It was unthinkable to so many that my daughter, Elisa, became such a zealous member of the Bund deutscher Mädel *in 1936.*

Few knew how terribly she suffered when the Red Cross informed us that Heinz had died in Dachau. The Germans were aware of Heinz's socialist leanings and looked for any reason to rid the world of him. Word got through to us that Heinz was shot in the legs and then hung by his feet in freezing weather for continuing to play chess while Hitler's speech was being broadcast in the Dachau bunkhouses.

Shortly after Heinz was taken, Elisa learned that her beloved professor Herr Doktor Kai Kahn had been killed in the street, in front of his apartment.

Even I was surprised to see Elisa strut about in the navy-blue-and-white uniform of the Bund deutscher Mädel. *But I did not discuss her newly found patriotism with her or try to discourage her. I knew she had suffered those losses, and I was sure she was terrified too, for the Nazi government had no one to answer to. On whim they took away whomever they wanted to. Your fine citizen Reinhardt Schwitter was killed in Dachau finally too. Rumors were that for a time he was made to play his violin for those in line to be gassed. Then it was his turn.*

At the time I thought maybe Elisa is right: Break

with any Jews, friends of Jews, sympathizers, even those with dichotomous surnames. Better to join the Nazis than to be harassed by them, possibly killed.

What I did not understand was my daughter. I had no inkling that she was this brave, courageous child who had on her own made contact with the resistance. Posing as a loyal member of the Bund deutscher Mädel, *she did underground work for a partisan organization involved in hiding Jews and undermining the everyday functioning of the Reich.*

I had no knowledge of that affiliation, for those courageous people could not even confide in the ones closest to them. I am not even sure today exactly when she joined the resistance. I believe she made contact with them through her old professor, Kai Kahn, just before they shot him. She was growing increasingly cautious about things. I remember how she disapproved of our having the Schwitters by to see if we had space for their Beckstein piano. I expected her father to reprimand her, but he did not, and often I wonder if he knew something about her plan or even assisted her. She could never do anything to give away her position. Therefore I never knew the courage of my beloved only child.

She was killed in 1942, by then operating as a courier for a resistance group hiding in the forest not far from my mother's home in Potsdam. Of course she knew those woods very well from playing there as a child.

I do not have and do not want the exact details of her death. I did, however, receive just last winter a small bundle of her belongings from someone who was able to track me down here in Aniane. There were not many things there, but all your letters were saved.

I thought you might like to have them, and they are enclosed. I also felt obliged to write you, so you know finally what became of Elisa.

May God bless you and your family.

Sincerely,

Sophie Stadler Leblanc

September 29, 1946

Dear Mrs. Leblanc,

I am so very sorry to learn details of Heinz Stadler's death, and of course my beloved Elisa's.

Dieter Schwitter, Wolfgang's younger brother, is my Verlobter, *so I knew about Reinhardt Schwitter's murder by the Nazis. I thank you very much for writing me about Elisa and for sending the letters I wrote to her.*

I thought of her always as my dearest friend, even though we knew each other for such a short time. I do not think I would be at Cornell University now, earning my Ph.D. in English literature, if our paths had never crossed. It was Elisa who taught me to love language, poetry, and literature. She was the one I always thought of as "the teacher," and now I am set on my own path to becoming a teacher myself, and perhaps a writer. Elisa used to tell me I told "sensational" stories. She was such a good listener too.

Elisa would have liked to know that our friend Richard Nolan declared himself a conscientious objector rather than fight in any war, and he was in a CO camp doing civilian service without pay for four years. The first time Elisa and I went anywhere together, it was to the film All Quiet on the Western Front, *which as you know is about a pacifist.*

My brother, Seth, was killed fighting in the Pacific in 1942. We feel fortunate that we have his